MAIGRET

AND THE TAVERN

BY THE SEINE

MAIGRET AND THE TAVERN BY THE SEINE

Georges Simenon

Translated from the French by
Geoffrey Sainsbury

A Harvest/HBJ Book
A Helen and Kurt Wolff Book
Harcourt Brace Jovanovich, Publishers
San Diego New York London

Requests for permission to make copies of any part of the work should be mailed to:
Permissions Department,
Harcourt Brace Jovanovich, Publishers,
Orlando, Florida 32887.

Library of Congress Cataloging-in-Publication Data
Simenon, Georges, 1903–1989.
[Guinguette à deux sous. English]
Maigret and the tavern by the Seine/
Georges Simenon; translated from the French by Geoffrey Sainsbury.
p. cm.
Translation of: La Guinguette à deux sous.
"A Helen and Kurt Wolff book."
ISBN 0-15-655164-0 (pbk.)
I. Title.
PQ2637.I53G813 1990 843'.912—dc20 90-36800

Printed in the United States of America

First Harvest/HBJ edition 1990

A B C D E

1

A Flat-brimmed Top-hat

A radiant late afternoon. An almost treacly sunshine oozing through the peaceful streets on the left bank of the Seine. An easygoing gaiety shining in every face and echoing in each familiar sound.

There are days like that. Days when existence is less commonplace than usual, days when trivial gestures seem somehow charged with vitality, and passersby on the pavement or passengers in trams are invested with some heightened personality.

It was the 27th of June. When Maigret reached the gate of the Santé he found the policeman on guard gazing foolishly at a little white cat which was playing with the dog from the dairy over the way.

There are days when footsteps strike a more

sonorous note. Maigret's did, as he crossed the immense courtyard to disappear through a doorway on the other side.

At the end of a long corridor he asked a warder:

"Has he been told?"

"Not yet."

A key turned in a lock. A bolt shot back. A very clean cell with a very high ceiling. A man, who rose to his feet, while from his face he seemed uncertain what expression to adopt.

"Well, Lenoir? You all right?"

The prisoner nearly smiled, but his features hardened as an idea flashed through his mind. He frowned mistrustfully, and for a few seconds his mouth was drawn into a snarl; then he shrugged his shoulders and held out his hand.

"I see," he said.

"What?"

A cynical smile.

"Come on! You needn't play that game with me. If you've come, it's . . ."

"It's because I'm going on leave tomorrow, and . . ."

Lenoir laughed dryly. He was tall and young, with dark hair combed back from the forehead, well-cut features, and fine chestnut-colored eyes. His neat black mustache showed up the whiteness of his teeth, which were sharp as a rodent's.

"Very kind of you, *Monsieur le commissaire. . . .*"

He stretched, yawned, and put down the lid

of the lavatory pan, which stood gaping in a corner of the cell.

"I wasn't expecting visitors. . . ."

Then suddenly, looking Maigret straight in the eye:

"They've turned it down, haven't they?"

No use trying to break the news gently. He had understood. He started pacing up and down the cell.

"I knew they would. . . . So when is it? . . . Tomorrow?"

All the same, the voice faltered ever so slightly over that last word, and the eyes greedily drank in the daylight that came through the narrow window high up on the wall.

At the same moment, people sitting in front of the cafés were scanning their evening papers, in which it was announced:

The President of the Republic has refused his consent to the reprieve of Jean Lenoir, the young ringleader of the Belleville gang. The execution will take place at dawn tomorrow.

It was Maigret himself who, three months before, had put his hand on Lenoir in a hotel in the Rue Saint-Antoine. It had been touch and go. Another second, and the gangster's revolver would have been pointing at the pit of his stomach instead of at the floor.

That, however, was all in the day's work, and the inspector bore him no grudge. On the contrary, he had taken rather a fancy to him. Partly because Lenoir was young. No more than twenty-two, though he had been sentenced heaven knows how often since his fifteenth birthday. But still more because he was game.

The crime had not been done single-handed. Two others of the gang had, in fact, probably played a more active part in the holdup than he had. They had both been arrested.

But Lenoir had taken the whole thing on his own shoulders. The police had tried to get at him from every angle, but he had steadily refused to rise to any bait.

And there was no pose about him, no swagger. Nor did he take the pathetic line and blame circumstances or social injustice for his own misdemeanors.

"You win!" was all he'd said.

Now it was all over. Or rather it soon would be. That sun which streaked diagonally across one of the cell walls had only to peep over the horizon next morning. . . .

And, in spite of himself, Lenoir's hand felt the back of his neck. His face turned a shade paler.

"It doesn't feel too good," he sneered.

Then, in a sudden outburst of rancor:

"If only all the others came too. There are plenty who deserve it just as much as I do."

Still walking up and down, he shot a shrewd glance at Maigret.

"All right! No need to prick up your ears! I'm not giving anybody away. . . . Not but what I wouldn't like to. . . ."

Maigret avoided looking at him. He could feel the confession coming, but he knew very well that Lenoir would shy off at the least thing—a word of misplaced sympathy or the slightest display of eager interest.

"Of course you wouldn't know the *Guinguette à Deux Sous.* . . . One of those riverside places where you can sit and booze in the garden. Just like any other *guinguette,* for that matter. No reason why you should know it. But if you ever fetch up there, you'll run into someone who'd fit just as well as I shall on that machine of yours tomorrow. . . ."

Quite unable to keep still, he went on pacing up and down. It was the only sign of his inward commotion. Maigret was fascinated.

"But you won't. . . . And you'll never catch him. . . . Look here! Without spilling any beans I can tell you a little story. . . . I don't know why it comes back to me all of a sudden. Perhaps because it belongs to the days when I was new to the business. I suppose I was about sixteen. . . . There were two of us. We used to go round the bars and cheap dancing-places together. My pal's in a sanatorium now—that is, if he's still alive. He was coughing his lungs up even in those days."

Why was he saying all this? Perhaps he needed to talk, to prove he was still alive himself, to prove he was still a man. . . .

"One night—it must have been about one o'clock . . . we were strolling along a street—

just an ordinary street: you don't need to know the name. . . . Some distance ahead a door opened. There was a car standing by the curb. And a guy came out of the house, pushing another in front of him. No, pushing's the wrong word. Imagine a guy arm-in-arm with a tailor's dummy, or as if he was giving a helping hand to a fellow who was soused. . . . He shoved him into the back of the car, and then took the wheel. . . .

"I caught my pal's eye, and by the time the car had started the two of us were on the rear bumper. They used to call me 'the cat,' and it wasn't a bad name either. . . .

"Well, off we drove. The fellow took us all over the shop. Seemed to be looking for something. More than once he turned and went back. But as soon as he struck the Canal Saint-Martin we tumbled to it. I don't need to tell you what he was up to the time he opened the door and shut it again; and the carcass was in the ditch. . . .

"A nice clean job. That bird's pockets must have been full of lead, for he didn't float a second. The only thing that rather spoilt it was our being there.

"A wink from Victor, and we were hanging on to the car again. We thought the fellow would be a nice one to have the address of. He stopped in the Place de la République, where there was a café still open, and swallowed down a glass of rum. Then he put his car away in a garage and went home. We saw a light go on in one of the flats, so we had no difficulty in finding him again. . . .

"For two years we squeezed him, Victor and me. We were new to it, and we were frightened of asking too much. . . . A few hundred francs at a time, no more. . . .

"Then one day we found he'd flown. Clean gone. We couldn't find a trace of him. . . . And then—would you believe it?—if I didn't run slap into him at the *Guinguette à Deux Sous.* That was three months ago—and the guy didn't even recognize me."

Lenoir spat. Automatically he put a hand to his pocket for a cigarette.

"When a guy's in my place," he muttered, "they might at least let him smoke!"

Maigret was staring at the bed. In a voice that was as indifferent as he could make it he asked:

"But you never knew who it was—the man whose body . . . ?"

"Funnily enough, we did. But there's no need for me to tell you."

The ray of sunshine had disappeared from the wall. Steps could be heard approaching in the corridor.

"Don't think I'm wanting to make myself out any better than I am. But that guy I've been talking about would do very well in my place on the . . ."

They almost spurted out: beads of sweat on Lenoir's forehead. His legs went limp. He sat down on the edge of the bed.

"You'd better leave me," he sighed. "Or

rather, no! . . . Perhaps I could do with a bit of company today. Better keep talking. . . . Would you like me to tell you about Marcelle? The woman who . . ."

The door opened. The condemned man's lawyer hesitated at the sight of Maigret. He had twisted his face into a professional smile. He was wondering how to break it gently to his client that his last hope had gone.

"I just looked in to talk things over . . ." he began evasively.

"You can chuck that!" snapped Lenoir.

Then to Maigret:

"Good-by, *Monsieur le commissaire.* I don't suppose we'll be seeing much more of each other. . . . No hard feelings: everybody to his trade. . . . And, by the way, I shouldn't waste time looking for that fellow. Even if you found him, he's probably as smart as you are by this time. . . ."

Maigret held out his hand. He saw the man's nostrils quiver. There were beads of sweat on the little black mustache too, and two sharp canines were biting into the lower lip.

"One way or another," said Lenoir with a forced laugh. "What does it matter? This way . . . or typhoid. . . ."

Maigret didn't go away, after all. At the last moment his holiday was postponed by a ticklish case concerning forged bonds. He was at it night and day and hadn't much time to think of the *Guinguette à Deux Sous.* All the same, he didn't forget it, and one day at the Quai des Orfèvres he mentioned the place to one of his colleagues.

"On the Seine, you say? Never heard of it. Would it be upstream or downstream?"

But Maigret couldn't even tell him that much.

Lenoir had been sixteen at the time, or so he'd said. That would make it six years ago. And one evening when Maigret was waiting for a report to come in, he whiled away the time turning over the criminal records of that year.

People had disappeared, as they always did. The only sensational case was that of a woman's body cut in pieces, the head of which was never found. As for the Canal Saint-Martin, it had produced a crop of six corpses that year.

The forged bonds gave more and more trouble, and then, when the case was finally wound up, the inspector hurried off to Alsace with Madame Maigret, who always spent one of the summer months there with her sister.

He only spent a couple of days there himself, but he promised to take his holiday as soon as possible—or at any rate a weekend.

Day by day, Paris emptied. The asphalt grew softer and softer under foot. Pedestrians chose the shady side of the street, and the terraces of the cafés were full to overflowing.

A fortnight slipped by, and Maigret was still pottering about, squaring up the arrears of work that had accumulated during the forged bonds case. At last Madame Maigret sent a telegram:

Expecting you without fail Sunday. Love from all.

So on Saturday—it was the 26th of July—he tidied up his desk, and told them in the office that he'd be out of town till late Monday night.

As he picked up his bowler, his eye lighted on the brim where the ribbon was worn through. As a matter of fact, it had been like that for weeks, and Madame Maigret had told him at least half a dozen times to buy a new one.

"If you go about like that much longer, they'll be giving you pennies in the street."

Catching sight of a hatter's in the Boulevard Saint-Martin, he went in, and began trying on bowlers, all of which were too small for him.

"You'll find this one just right, sir," the measly little shop-assistant kept repeating.

Maigret was never more unhappy than when trying on clothes. In utter misery he stared into the glass, waiting for more bowlers to be brought him.

Behind him, in the mirror, he could see a man's back, and a head on which was perched a rather old-fashioned top-hat. As the man was in rough tweeds, the effect was decidedly ridiculous.

"Haven't you anything older still? I'm not really going to wear it. . . ."

Gloomily Maigret wondered how much longer he was to be kept waiting.

"It's only a joke. The whole thing's a rag. We're staging a village marriage at a place we go to, the *Guinguette à Deux Sous*. Just between friends—and we're all taking a part. Bride, bridesmaids, and all the rest of it. I'm to be the mayor. So you see the style of thing I want?"

The customer chuckled. He was a man about thirty-five, hale and hearty, who would be taken anywhere for a prosperous business man.

"For instance, if you had one with a flat brim . . ."

"I think we've got just the thing you want. If you wouldn't mind waiting a moment, I'll go up to the workshop."

Another pile of bowlers. The first Maigret tried fitted him perfectly, but he was no longer in a hurry. In fact, he only made his final choice just in time to follow the other customer out of the shop. He hailed a passing taxi, in case it should be necessary.

It was. For the other dived into a car that was standing by the side of the road, started it up, and drove off towards the Rue Vielle-du-Temple.

Here he stopped at a secondhand shop. Old clothes and bric-à-brac. The typical *brocanteur*. It was half an hour before he emerged with a large flat cardboard box which obviously contained the suit that was to go with the flat-brimmed top-hat.

The Champs-Elysées, then the Avenue de Wagram. The next stop was at a little bar at a street corner, where he only spent a bare five minutes, returning to the car accompanied by a jolly-faced, buxom little woman who by her looks was just on the right side of thirty.

Twice Maigret had looked at his watch. He had already missed the train he'd intended catching. And now the next would be leaving in a quarter of an hour. But he shrugged his shoulders and answered the driver's enquiring look with:

"Go on. Keep them in sight."

It was pretty well what he expected: the car stopped next in front of a tall building in the Avenue Niel. The couple disappeared through the entrance. After waiting a quarter of an hour, Maigret followed, reading as he passed the words on the brass plate:

Bachelor apartments by the month or by the day.

A perfumed manageress was sitting in the little office, which smelt of middle-class adultery.

"*Police Judiciaire!* . . . The couple that's just gone in? . . ."

"What couple?"

But she soon gave up stalling.

"Most respectable people—both of them married. They come twice a week."

When he went out, the inspector looked through the car window at the little brass plate, the *plaque d'identité*, that bears the owner's name and address.

Marcel Basso
32 Quai d'Austerlitz
Paris

* * *

The warm air was stagnant. The buses and trams that fed the stations were packed. Taxis had deck-chairs on their roofs, fishing-rods protruding from their windows, and a heap of luggage by the driver's side.

The glistening asphalt reflected a bluish light. At every café terrace a clatter of saucers. . . .

"Exactly four weeks," mused Maigret, "since Lenoir was . . ."

It hadn't aroused much interest. Just an everyday matter—a professional criminal meeting a professional death. Maigret remembered his quivering nostrils and the neat little black mustache. He looked at his watch and sighed.

Too late now to think of joining his wife. She and her sister would walk down to meet the last train, and the latter would not fail to mutter:

"There you are! Always the same!"

The taxi-driver was reading a paper. The top-hat customer came out first, looking to see the coast was clear before beckoning to his companion, who remained inside.

They stopped in the Place des Ternes. Through the rear window the couple could be seen kissing. Then the woman hailed a passing taxi and jumped in, only letting go of the man's hand at the very last moment.

The car drove on.

"Do you still want me to follow?"

"You may as well, while you're about it."

It wasn't very interesting. But at any rate he'd

found somebody who knew the *Guinguette à Deux Sous*.

Quai d'Austerlitz. A huge board, on which was painted:

Marcel Basso
Coal and Coke Merchant and Importer
Wholesale and Retail
Special Summer Prices

A yard surrounded by a blackened fence. Opposite, on the other side of the road, there were cranes on the quay, barges lying alongside, and another board bearing Marcel Basso's name. A heap of coal that had just been unloaded. . . . To one side of the coal-merchant's yard stood a large private house in villa style. Monsieur Basso parked his car, looked down to make sure there was no hair or powder on his clothes and went in.

Maigret next caught sight of him through a wide-open window on the first floor. He was with a tall, fair, good-looking woman. They were talking eagerly and laughing. Monsieur Basso tried on the top-hat again in front of the glass.

They seemed to be packing. A white-aproned maid kept coming in and out of the room.

A quarter of an hour later—it had gone five—the whole household appeared at the front door. First of all a boy of ten, carrying an airgun. Then the servant, Monsieur and Madame Basso, the gardener with the luggage.

The whole scene was brimming with good-humor. The whole of Paris, for that matter. Cars passed constantly, heading for the country. At the Gare de Lyons, where they were running double services, engines whistled wildly.

Madame Basso took the seat next her husband's. The boy got in at the back, with the luggage, and lowered both of the windows.

The car was nothing grand. Just a good, ordinary, dark blue car like a thousand others. It must have been purchased quite recently.

A few minutes later they were driving along towards Villeneuve-Saint-Georges, after which they took the Corbeil road. On the other side of Corbeil they turned off into a low-lying narrow road that ran beside the river.

Mon Loisir.

That's what it was called, the Bassos' villa, which overlooked a stretch of the river between Morsang and Seineport. A newly built house, the brickwork bright red, the paintwork unweathered. The flowers in the garden seemed to have been washed that morning.

A little white-painted jetty with a springboard. A couple of boats moored to the riverbank.

"Do you know this part?" Maigret asked the driver.

"A bit."

"Is there any place to put up at?"

"At the *Vieux Garçon*. That's in Morsang. . . . And there's a place in Seineport. *Chez Marins*—I think that's the name."

"And the *Guinguette à Deux Sous?*"

The driver shook his head. Never heard of it.

The taxi couldn't stay there much longer without attracting attention. The Bassos' car had already disgorged its load. In less than ten minutes after their arrival Madame Basso appeared in the garden in sailor clothes of red-brown canvas, or *toile de Concarneau,* and an American sailor cap.

Her husband, on the other hand, was in a hurry to get into his fancy-dress. He appeared at a window, buttoned up in an impossible frock-coat and with the flat-brimmed top-hat on his head.

"What do you say to that?" he called out.

"You haven't forgotten the sash, I hope?"

"What sash?"

"Doesn't a mayor wear a red-white-and-blue sash, silly? . . ."

Boats glided by lazily on the river. Far away in the distance a tug blew a long blast on its siren. The sun was just sinking into the trees on the hill downstream.

"Make it the *Vieux Garçon,*" said Maigret.

A dozen cars were parked to one side, while behind the inn was a wide terrace on the riverbank. Boats of every description in the water below.

"Do you want me to wait?"

"I'll let you know. . . ."

The first person he met was a woman, dressed all in white and with a wreath of orange-blossom on her head. She was running for all she was worth, and nearly went full tilt into the inspector. A young man in bathing-costume was chasing her. Both were convulsed with laughter.

Others in the garden were watching the scene. One shouted out:

"Now then! Don't go mauling the bride!"

"At any rate till the wedding's over," cried another.

The bride stopped, panting for breath, and Maigret at once recognized the lady who twice a week paid flying visits to the Avenue Niel accompanied by Monsieur Basso.

A man in a green rowing-boat was putting away his fishing-gear, his forehead wrinkled as though he was engaged on some difficult and arduous task.

Another young man came out of the inn, ordering drinks over his shoulder!

"Cinq Pernods. . . . Cinq. . . ."

His face was covered with greasepaint. He was got up to play the part of a course-grained, boisterous, spotty peasant.

"Do I look all right?"

"No. You ought to have had red hair."

A car drew up. The people who alighted were already dressed for the village wedding. One woman wore a puce silk dress which trailed along the ground. Her husband had stuffed a cushion under his waistcoat to give himself a paunch, while across it, in place of a watch-chain, lay a length of chain cable borrowed from a boat.

The sun's rays had turned red. Hardly a leaf stirred in the evening stillness.

"When are the carriages coming?"

Maigret wandered round, not knowing quite what to do with himself.

"What about the Bassos?"

"They overtook us on the road."

Suddenly Maigret found another member of the party standing right in front of him. A man in the early thirties, though already almost completely bald. A face like a clown's. A gleam of sardonic humor sparkled in his eye. When he spoke, it was with a strong English accent.

"Just the man we want!" he said, looking at Maigret.

"What for?" asked someone.

"What's he look like? . . . A notary, of course! No one seems to have thought of the marriage contract."

Then, turning to Maigret with the easy familiarity of a drunkard, he went on:

"You'll be our notary, won't you, old boy? . . . Come on. We're going to have a grand time. But first of all you must have a drink."

And he led Maigret off by the arm amid general laughter, while one woman muttered:

"Really! . . . James! . . . . He's got the cheek of the devil."

But James seemed to take it very easily in his stride. With an air of casual intimacy he swept Maigret indoors and into the bar.

Ten minutes later, Maigret found a pretext to sneak out and pay off his taxi.

2

The Wedding-feast

On his arrival at the *Guinguette à Deux Sous,* Maigret had only been mildly interested in what he was doing. The case hadn't clicked. Following Monsieur Basso, he had known that ten to one he was on a wild-goose chase. At the *Vieux Garçon* he had looked round him dully, without experiencing that sudden spurt of interest which meant that some intuitive nostril had picked up a trail.

Nor did his clinking glasses with James succeed in plunging him into the atmosphere of a case. The curtain hadn't gone up, and his spirit remained aloof as he watched the rest of the party assemble, while fresh costumes, each more absurd than the last, were proudly displayed to guffaws or splutterings of laughter.

The Bassos had joined up, their boy, as a carrot-haired village idiot, being the biggest hit of all.

"Don't worry about them," said James each time Maigret turned round. "They're happy enough—though they haven't had a dozen drinks between them!"

Two old-fashioned carriages drove up. More laughter, jostling, and nudging as the party scrambled in. Maigret took the seat that was offered him by James's side. The innkeeper, his wife, and all the servants crowded round the entrance to the *Vieux Garçon* to give them a suitable send-off.

The sunset had given place to a bluish twilight. On the other side of the river stood peaceful country-houses, whose lighted windows shimmered through the dusk.

The carriages trundled along the narrow road. Almost grudgingly, the inspector's eye took in the faces around him. The coachman, the butt of a good deal of raillery, who laughed back rather sourly; a girl made up as Bécassine, the proverbial little slavey, up from the country, who was practicing a local accent; a gray-haired gentleman, got up as a grandmother.

It was altogether a strange turnout, so unexpected as to be rather confusing. It was difficult to bring these people into focus, and Maigret could only make the vaguest of guesses as to what sort of people they were in everyday life.

"That's my wife, sitting over there," said James, pointing to the plumpest of the women, who wore exaggerated leg-of-mutton sleeves.

He said it in a voice of resignation, and the twinkle in his eye grew for a moment sad.

They sang. As they drove through Seineport, people rushed out on to their doorsteps to see them pass. Little boys ran after them, cheering and waving.

The drivers reined in, and they crossed the bridge at a walk. An innkeeper's signboard was just visible in the failing light.

Eugène Rougier—Débitant.

A tiny little house, all white, squeezed in between the towing-path and the hillside. The lettering on the signboard was primitive to a degree. As they came closer, they could hear snatches of music, punctuated by grinding and squeaking.

What was it that suddenly brought the "click"? Maigret couldn't have told you himself. Was it the little white house, so humble, with its two lighted windows, contrasting with this sudden farcical invasion?

Or was it the couple that came forward to inspect the wedding-party? The man was a young factory-hand. With him a pretty girl in a pink silk dress, her hands on her hips. . . .

The house itself was really no more than a good-sized cottage of two rooms with the front door between them. In the room on the right, an old woman was fussing round the kitchen range. In the one on the left, Maigret caught a glimpse of a bed and some family portraits.

The bar was behind. Nothing more than a large lean-to with one side completely open on to the garden. Tables and benches. A bar. An automatic piano. Lanterns.

Some bargees were drinking at the bar. A twelve-year-old girl was looking after the automatic piano, winding it up every few minutes and putting two sous in the slot.

Yes. Whatever it was, something had clicked and the case was on. The case of the *Guinguette à Deux Sous.*

The place was soon bubbling over with exuberance. The newcomers were no sooner out of the carriages than they cleared away the tables and started dancing. Others called for drinks. Maigret lost sight of James for a moment, but he soon caught sight of him at the bar, leaning pensively over a Pernod.

There were also tables under the trees in the garden. A waiter was laying them. The driver of one of the carriages sighed as he said to his mate:

"Let's hope they won't keep it up all night. . . ."

"Not much use hoping," answered the other. "It's Saturday."

Maigret was left to himself. Standing all alone, he slowly turned round and surveyed his surroundings: the little house with smoke pouring out of one of the chimneys, the two carriages, the shed behind, the factory-hand out with his best girl, the dressed-up crowd of merrymakers.

"That's it, all right," he grunted to himself.

A riverside inn with a garden—*une guinguette. La Guinguette à Deux Sous. . . .* Would that refer to the poverty of the place? Or to the two sous you had to put in the old bumble-jar when you wanted some music?

And it was the haunt of a murderer. Had been, at any rate. Was he still hanging about? That factory-hand? A bargee? Or even one of the party?

James, for instance, or Monsieur Basso?

There was no electric light. The shed was lit up by two oil-lanterns, and others stood on the tables in the garden. So, when night fell, the scene was divided up into patches of light and darkness.

Dinner was ready, and the cry went up:

"A table! . . . On mange! . . ."

But the words had little effect. The dancing went on, while those at the bar ordered fresh drinks. Another round, a third, a fourth, and by the time the company were seated the majority of them were well under way.

The innkeeper's wife brought on the food and served it herself, enquiring anxiously whether it was all right—the soup, the omelette, the rabbit. But nobody bothered to answer her. As a matter of fact, what with talking, laughing, and drinking, few had any idea whether they were eating good food or bad.

The noise they made drowned the automatic piano that was still being fed with coins, and the voices of the bargees who conversed phlegmatically about the canals of Northern France and Belgium and the electric haulage that was being introduced at many of the locks.

The factory-hand and his girl were the only couple dancing now. They danced cheek to cheek, but their eyes constantly returned to the uproarious wedding-feast.

Not a soul Maigret knew, not a face he had ever set eyes on before. On one side of him was a woman made up preposterously with a faint mustache—and not so faint as all that—and beauty-spots dotted about all over her face. She had promptly christened him Uncle Arthur.

"Pass the salt, Uncle Arthur. . . ."

They called each other by their Christian names, they dug each other in the ribs to attract attention, or kicked each other under the table. Were they really such intimate friends? Or just a crowd of people that had been thrown together by chance?

And what would they be in ordinary life? Maigret's thoughts kept on reverting to that question. The man dressed up as a grandmother, for instance—what might he be?

Or the woman disguised as a flapper, who spoke all the time in a falsetto voice?

Well-to-do middle-class people, like Monsieur Basso—that seemed the most likely answer. Still, it was impossible to tell.

Monsieur Basso sat beside the bride. He kept his hands off her scrupulously, but now and again he gave her a meaning look whose significance Maigret was possibly the only one to guess:

"We had a grand time this afternoon, didn't we?"

Avenue Niel. Bachelor apartments for middle-class adultery. . . .

Would her husband be amongst the party? . . .

Someone let off a squib. Then Bengal lights flared up under the trees. The dancing couple stopped and, hand-in-hand, stared tenderly at the brightly colored flames. And the girl exclaimed:

"It's just like a play."

Yet it was the haunt of a murderer!

"Speech! . . . Speech! . . . Speech! . . ."

With a delighted smile on his lips, Monsieur Basso rose. He bowed, he hemmed and hawed, feigning embarrassment, and finally began a rambling discourse, full of absurdities and pompous platitudes, punctuated by thunders of applause.

Only, now and again, his eye fell on Maigret's face, the only grave face at the table. And each time, Monsieur Basso's eye passed on with a flicker of embarrassment that was no longer put on.

And yet, after a moment, he couldn't help looking back once more.

". . . and I must ask you, ladies and gentlemen, to raise your glasses and join me in the toast: *Vive la Mariée!*"

And everyone but Maigret shouted:

"Vive la Mariée!"

Everyone was standing now. Glasses were clinked. Kisses were showered on the bride. With that the feast was over and the dancing started again.

Maigret saw Monsieur Basso go up to James and ask him something—in all probability:

"Who is he?"

The answer was audible.

"I don't know. . . . Just a pal . . . a rattling good fellow."

The abandoned tables looked desolate now. The shed, on the other hand, was packed with dancers. Little by little, quite a crowd had gathered round to watch the spectacle, dim figures in the darkness, hardly distinguishable from the tree trunks.

Champagne corks popped.

"Come and have a brandy," said James. "I take it you're not a dancer."

A queer chap. He had drunk enough in the course of the evening to lay out five strong men, yet he wasn't really drunk. He slouched along in a desultory way and with an air of detachment, leading Maigret into the kitchen, where he sat down in the landlord's high-backed armchair.

The latter's wife was bustling to and fro.

"Eugène! Here! . . . They've ordered another six bottles of bubbly. You'd better get one of the drivers to fetch some more from Corbeil."

A middle-aged woman, getting on for fifty. The old woman with the rounded back, who was washing up, was obviously her mother.

A typical cottage interior, very poor indeed. A grandfather clock in carved walnut. . . . And James took the bottle of cognac he had ordered and filled two glasses to the brim. Then, stretching out his legs, he leaned back in his chair.

"Here's to you! . . ."

They couldn't see the dancing, but they could hear it. At that distance the sound had fused into a compact mass of talk, laughter, music, and the slip of feet. Out through the open door, invisible in the night, the Seine flowed by.

"What a place!" sneered James. "Everything the heart can desire, including plenty of dark corners to cuddle in."

There was something about James which told you he was not the man to steal a kiss in a dark corner.

"I don't mind betting they're at it already at the bottom of the garden."

He watched the old grandmother, bent over the basin of water.

"Come on! Let's have a cloth."

And with a casual air, but with careful movements, he patiently dried the pile of plates and glasses, only stopping from time to time to take a gulp of brandy.

Now and again someone passed the door. Maigret took advantage of a moment when James was talking to the old grandmother, and slipped out. He hadn't taken ten steps outside when someone asked him for a light. It was the gray-haired man in woman's clothes.

"Thanks. Don't you dance either?"

"Never."

"Not like my wife. She hasn't stopped for a second."

And with a sudden intuition, Maigret asked:

"The bride?"

"Yes. And if she stands about afterwards, she'll be sure to catch cold."

He sighed. He was absurd, with his middle-aged man's face over an old lady's tight bodice and full skirt.

Once more Maigret wondered what he did for a living, and what he looked like in his everyday clothes. To sound him, he asked:

"I can't help feeling we've met before. . . ."

"I was just thinking the same. Where could it have been? . . . Or perhaps you've come to my shop. A hosier's on the Grands Boulevards. . . ."

"Perhaps. . . ."

His wife was making more noise than any two others. She was as tight as a lord. She was dancing with Basso, and was clinging to him in such a way that Maigret turned his head away.

"A queer little girl," sighed her husband.

Little girl, indeed! A full-bodied woman of twenty-eight or nine, with sensual lips and a challenging eye, who seemed utterly abandoned to her partner.

"When she once gets going, she's altogether wild," sighed her husband.

Maigret looked hard at him. Was the hosier angry with his wife or proud of her?

Suddenly there were shouts. The party was being called together for the final ceremony of conducting the married couple to the bridal chamber. There was a hunt for the bridegroom, who was at last discovered at the far end of the garden.

The bridal chamber was a little outhouse beyond the shed. The door was opened. Maigret kept one eye on the real husband, who looked on, smiling.

"First of all, the garter . . ." said someone.

The rite was observed. It was Monsieur Basso who removed it, cut it into small pieces, handing one to each member of the gang as a souvenir. Then bride and bridegroom were pushed into the outhouse and the door was locked.

"She loves a game of this sort," said the hosier. "Are you married too?"

"Me? . . . Yes."

"But your wife's not here, is she?"

"No. She's away in the country."

"Does she like young people too?"

Maigret couldn't make out whether the other was pulling his leg or speaking seriously. A minute or two later he slipped away. Crossing the garden, he saw the factory-hand and his girl standing behind a tree bush, locked in each other's arms.

In the kitchen, James was still drying glasses, while he never stopped emptying others. At the same time he was having a quiet, homely chat with the old grandmother.

"What are they up to now?" he asked Maigret. "Have you seen my wife?"

"I didn't notice her."

"She's fat enough."

The end came almost abruptly. It must have been round about one in the morning. Someone whispered to his neighbor that it was time to think of going. The neighbor said the same to someone else. A man was being sick near the riverbank. The bride and bridegroom had long ago been released. Only a few of the younger ones were still dancing.

One of the drivers went to find James.

"Are you going to be much longer? My old woman's been expecting me for the last hour, and . . ."

"Oh! So you're married too?"

James gave the signal. The party was rounded up, and the carriages trundled homewards. Some nodded in their seats, while others kept the ball rolling, singing and laughing, though with ebbing gusto.

They passed a group of sleeping barges. Far off a train whistled.

The Bassos were put down at their door. The hosier and his wife had already been dropped at Seineport. A woman was scolding her drunken husband in an undertone:

"I'll tell you about it tomorrow. I saw what

you did. . . . It's no use arguing. I simply shan't listen. . . ."

The sky was studded with stars, which were reflected by the river. At the *Vieux Garçon*, all was asleep. Handshakes all round.

"Sailing tomorrow?"

"I think we're going fishing."

"Good night."

A long passage. A row of bedrooms. Maigret asked James:

"Is there one for me? I didn't book one. . . ."

"Take any. The first empty one you come to. If you don't find one, you can share mine."

Lights were switched on. Boots and shoes thrown on the floor. Bed-springs creaking. Lights switched off.

A lot of loud whispering in one of the rooms. No doubt the woman who had something to tell her husband. . . .

It was eleven o'clock in the morning, the day hot and sunny. The party had reverted once more to their normal selves, and Maigret had no longer to make an effort to see through their disguise. Waitresses in black dresses and white aprons bustled about on the terrace laying the tables.

People lounged in deck-chairs or wandered from group to group. Some were still in pyjamas, some in sailor trousers, the remainder being for the most part in flannels.

"Mouth like the bottom of a parrot-cage?"

"Not so bad as all that. What about yours?"

Some were away fishing; others had already returned. Some were sailing, some were rowing.

The hosier was in a well-cut gray flannel suit. Obviously a man who set great store by being well groomed. Seeing Maigret, he walked up to him.

"Allow me to introduce myself—Monsieur Feinstein. . . . I mentioned my shop yesterday, but I trade under the name of Marcel."

"Did you have a good night?"

"Anything but! As I expected, my wife was taken ill. It's the same every time. And she knows perfectly well she has a weak heart."

He wasn't altogether natural. He seemed to be watching for Maigret's reactions as he went on:

"Have you seen her this morning?"

He looked round, finally spotting her in a sailing-boat with four or five others dressed in bathing-costumes. Monsieur Basso was at the helm.

"Is this your first visit to Morsang? A charming spot. It'll grow on you—you'll see. We have the place practically to ourselves. The same crowd come every weekend. Do you play bridge?"

"A bit."

"We shall be playing later on. You know Monsieur Basso, I suppose? One of the biggest coal-merchants in Paris. Such a nice fellow. That's his own boat he's sailing. His wife's wild about every kind of sport."

"And James?"

"I bet he's having a Pernod—and not his first

either. It's all he lives for. Dreadful when it catches them so young. . . . He could have made a career for himself if he'd taken the trouble. He works in an English bank in the Place Vendôme. Plenty of better jobs have been offered him, but he's always turned them down. No ambition whatever. They finish work at the bank at five, and that suits him down to the ground. The rest of the day, he's bar-crawling. You can generally find him in one of the cafés in the Rue Royale. . . ."

"And that young chap—the tall one?"

"Son of a jeweler."

"And the man fishing over there?"

"A builder. He's the keenest fisherman of the lot. Fishing, boating, swimming, bridge . . . those are the chief occupations here. We're a very happy family. Most of them stay here, but a few of us have our own villas or bungalows. Ours is at Seineport."

A long stretch of the river was visible, and just where it turned was the little white house, behind which was the shed with the automatic piano.

"Do you often go to the *Guinguette à Deux Sous?*"

"Yes. We've been going there for nearly two years now. It was a discovery of James's. Before that, it was only frequented by bargees and the working-class people of Corbeil, who used to dance there on Sundays. The sort of place James likes. He used to slink off there all by himself when he was fed up with the others. Then one day they found him there. And they started dancing, and somehow the place took on. So much so that we've pretty well bought the place up. Not many of the old customers go there now. . . ."

A waitress passed with a tray loaded with drinks. The splash of someone diving into the river. A smell of frying floated from the kitchen.

And there, at the bend of the river, a column of smoke rose from the chimney of the little white house. Maigret thought of Jean Lenoir! the little black mustache, the sharp teeth, the quivering nostrils. Jean Lenoir, who had tried to walk his feelings off by pacing up and down his cell. What was it he had said?

"If only all the others came too. There are plenty that deserved it just as much as I do."

But the next morning he had been alone. Nobody had kept him company. Nobody from the *Guinguette à Deux Sous. . . .*

And in spite of the midday summer heat Maigret was conscious of a sudden chill, and it was with different eyes that he looked at this well-groomed hosier smoking a gold-tipped cigarette. Then he turned towards the boat which Basso was just bringing alongside. Its half-naked occupants jumped ashore and gaily greeted the others.

"May I introduce you?" said Feinstein. "I'm afraid I don't know your name. . . . Monsieur . . . ?"

"Maigret, *fonctionnaire. . .*"

An official. He hadn't lied. The business was gone through quite ceremoniously. There were bows and murmurs of *"enchanté"* and *"tout le plaisir est pour moi."*

"You were with us last night, weren't you? It went off splendidly, don't you think so? Will you be joining in the bridge this afternoon?"

A thin young man plucked Monsieur Feinstein by the sleeve and drew him aside. A whispered conversation followed that was not lost on Maigret. The hosier's face clouded, then a frightened look came into it. Furtively, he eyed the inspector from head to foot. It cost him an effort to regain his composure.

The whole group had wandered over to the tables on the terrace.

"What are we having? . . . Pernods all round? Hello! Where's James?"

In spite of the effort he was making, Monsieur Feinstein could not altogether hide his nervousness. He redoubled his attentions to Maigret.

"Is that all right for you? . . . A Pernod?"

"Anything you like. It's all the same to me."

"You're not . . . ?" began Feinstein, but he thought better of it and broke off, staring hard at the other bank of the river as though something had attracted his attention. Then he tried again from another angle:

"It's odd you should have stumbled on Morsang. . . ."

"Yes, it's odd," Maigret agreed.

The drinks were served. Conversation struck

up on all sides. Madame Feinstein's foot was touching Monsieur Basso's and her bright eyes were fixed on him almost continuously.

"A lovely day. But, of course, it spoils the fishing. The water's too clear. . . ."

The air was sultry and rather oppressive. Maigret's thoughts reverted to Lenoir's cell and the ray of sunshine striking high up on the wall. And Lenoir had walked and walked, as though to forget that he soon would walk no more.

Maigret's eye fell weightily on each in turn of the people sitting round him. On Monsieur Basso, the hosier, the builder, on young men and young women, and lastly on James, who at that moment came up to join them.

One after the other he tried to picture them by the Canal Saint-Martin, pitching a weighted body into the water.

"Your health!" said Monsieur Feinstein, with his most engaging smile.

3

Behind the "Guinguette"

Maigret had lunch on the terrace at a table by himself. But the others were all round him and the conversation was general. He had them pretty well placed by now. The bulk of them were shopkeepers, small manufacturers, and so on. The only ones not in business were an engineer and a doctor.

They were not rich, but comfortably off. All worked for their living, and the Saturday afternoon and Sunday were the most any of them had in the way of leisure.

Practically every family had a boat of some sort, and almost all were more or less enthusiastic about fishing. Twenty-four hours a week they would lay their work aside to wander about in flannels or *toile de Concarneau*, barefoot or in sandals.

Everything nautical was fashionable here, and some of them even simulated the rolling gait of old sea-dogs. Some of the younger people were single, but the majority were married couples. Between them reigned that almost exaggerated familiarity which prevails in a common gang.

James was the most popular. In fact, in his casual, easygoing way, he even seemed to hold the gang together. Whenever he showed his brick-red face and dreamy eyes, there would be good-humored laughter and jocular back-chat.

"Here's James. How's things, James? Mouth like the bottom of a parrot-cage?"

"Never! If it's a bit sticky sometimes, it's soon cleaned up with a couple of Pernods. . . ."

The previous night's farce was the chief topic of conversation. The chap who'd been sick was teased unmercifully. So was another who had nearly fallen into the river.

Maigret was accepted as a member of the party. All the same, he didn't quite belong. The evening before, they had called him Uncle Arthur, while now they inspected him out of the corner of an eye. Not that he was left in the cold. Every now and again a phrase would be addressed to him out of politeness.

"Are you a fisherman too? . . ."

The Bassos were lunching at home. Indeed, all who had villas to go to had disappeared. It divided the gang into two sections: those who had villas, and those who stayed at the inn. The Feinsteins had a villa.

About two o'clock the hosier returned. He

went straight up to Maigret, whom he seemed to have taken under his wing.

"We're playing bridge at the Bassos'. They're expecting you too."

"Do you always play at their house?"

"No. In fact, it should have been at ours today. But our maid's ill, so we cried off. . . . Are you coming, James?"

"Yes. But I think I'll sail. There's a bit of a breeze again now."

The Bassos' villa was less than three-quarters of a mile upstream. Maigret and Feinstein went on foot. Others sailed or rowed, and one or two got their cars out.

"A delightful fellow, Basso. Don't you think so?"

Once again Maigret couldn't decide whether the man was sneering or whether he meant it.

Really he was a strange man. Strange in that he was so difficult to classify. He had no dominant feature. He was neither old nor young, not good-looking, not ugly. Altogether an unknown quantity. His head might be destitute of any trace of thought—or it might equally well be cram-full of dark secrets.

"I suppose you'll be coming every Sunday now?"

They passed groups of people who had been picnicking by the river, and every hundred yards or so a patient fisherman. In spite of a slight breeze, it seemed hotter than ever, so sultry as to be almost suffocating.

Wasps were buzzing round the flowers in the

Bassos' garden. Three cars were drawn up in front of the house. The boy was playing in the water.

"You're a bridge-player, I believe," said the coal-merchant, shaking Maigret's hand cordially. "That's splendid. We can start in right away without waiting for James. Heaven knows when he'll get here—trying to beat upstream on a day like this!"

The house was built and furnished in cottage style. Everything bright and clean as a new pin. Lots of windows, with red check curtains. Old Normandy furniture, and rustic pottery.

The card-table was in a sitting-room with a large bay window through which you could go straight into the garden. Bottles of *Vouvray* were standing in a silver ice-bucket whose surface was misty with condensation, and liqueurs had been put ready on a tray. Madame Basso, in her sailor clothes, looked after her guests.

"Will you have a liqueur? *Cognac, quetsch, mirabelle?* . . . Unless you'd rather have the *Vouvray?* . . ."

More introductions were necessary, as some of the Bassos' friends were not members of the gang.

"Monsieur . . . ?"

"Maigret."

"Monsieur Maigret. He plays bridge. So you've got a four. . . ."

The brightness and freshness of the place made it seem like a toy, or a scene in a musical comedy. There was nothing to remind one that life was a serious business. The boy was pushing off from the bank in a white-painted canoe, and his mother called out:

"Take care, Pierrot!"

"I'm only going to meet James."

"A cigar, Monsieur Maigret?" asked Basso. "Or, if you prefer a pipe, there's tobacco in the jar there. . . . Yes. Do by all means. My wife's used to it by now."

On the other side of the river stood the little white house—the *Guinguette à Deux Sous.*

The first part of the afternoon passed off uneventfully. Monsieur Basso didn't join in the bridge, but Maigret was able to notice that he seemed less at ease than in the morning. Was that because he was the host? He certainly didn't look the sort of man to be put off his stroke by a little thing like that. He was tall and heavily built, exuding vitality at every pore. Hale and hearty, a little coarse-grained, of plebeian fiber. . . .

Monsieur Feinstein took his bridge in earnest, and Maigret, who was his partner, earned more than one reproof.

Members of the Morsang gang were arriving all the time, and by four o'clock the house and garden were crowded. Someone put on the gramophone. Madame Basso handed round the *Vouvray*. Within a quarter of an hour there were half a dozen couples dancing round the bridge-players.

Monsieur Feinstein seemed completely absorbed in the game, and Maigret was surprised to hear him mutter:

"Hello! Where's our friend Basso got to?"

"I think he went off in a boat," said someone.

Following the hosier's eyes, Maigret saw a boat which had just reached the opposite bank, near the *Guinguette à Deux Sous*. Monsieur Basso jumped ashore and went up to the little inn. He soon reappeared, and in a short time had rejoined the party. He talked and laughed as heartily as ever, but Maigret couldn't help thinking he looked preoccupied.

Feinstein had already won two rubbers and looked like winning a third. His wife danced with Basso. James stood near the card-table, holding a glass of *Vouvray*.

"There are some that couldn't lose," he said, "even if they tried."

Was he jibing at the hosier? If he was, no one took any notice, and the hosier himself made no response. He was dealing, and Maigret noticed the steadiness and competence of his hands.

Another hour passed. The dancing was beginning to flag. Some of the guests had been bathing. James, who had taken Maigret's place at the bridge-table, had lost a rubber in quick time. He rose from his seat, saying:

"Time we had a change of scene. Who's for the *Guinguette à Deux Sous?*"

On his way out he noticed Maigret.

"Come along, you!"

He had reached the degree of intoxication which he never went beyond, no matter how much he drank. Others followed. A young man, using his hands as a megaphone bawled out:

"Everybody to the *Guinguette!*"

"That's the way," said James, helping Maigret into his boat.

He pushed off, sending the boat shooting into the stream. Then he lolled back in the stern-sheets, with one hand on the tiller.

But there was hardly a breath of wind now, hardly enough to enable the boat to stem the stream, though the latter ran lazily enough.

"It doesn't matter. There's no hurry."

Maigret saw Marcel Basso and Feinstein cross in a motorboat. They were on the other bank in no time, walking together up to the *Guinguette.*

Skiffs and dinghies followed. James had been the first to push off. Yet all the others had reached the other bank when he and Maigret were only halfway across. He might have used his oars, but didn't seem inclined to take the trouble.

"They're a good lot," he said, as though following some inward train of thought.

"Who?" asked Maigret, to draw him out.

"All of them. . . . They don't seem to know what to do with themselves. But that's not their fault, is it? Life's a boring business. . . ."

It sounded funny, because James, sprawling in the stern with the sun shining on his bald head, looked sublimely contented.

"Is it true you're a detective? . . ."
"Who told you so?"
"I don't know. But that's what they say. . . . Never mind. It's a trade, like any other."
A puff of wind filled the sail, and he gave a pull at the sheet. The clock at Morsang was striking six. Then the one at Seineport answered. Except in one or two places, the other bank of the river was overgrown with reeds, teeming with insects.
"What do you think of . . . ?" began James, but he was cut short by a sharp crack. At the same time, Maigret jumped to his feet, nearly overturning the boat.
"Look out!" shouted James, throwing his weight over to the other side to prevent the boat capsizing.
Then he seized one of the oars, put it over the stern and started sculling. His forehead was puckered and his eyes looked anxious.
"What could it be? . . . There's no shooting this month. . . ."
"It came from behind the *Guinguette*," said Maigret.
They were close to the bank now and could hear the automatic piano. then a terror-stricken voice screaming:
"Stop it! . . . Stop the music!"
Someone dashed through the dancers, and a moment later the music stopped abruptly. One couple, oblivious of the alarm, danced the whole length of the shed before breaking off. The old grandmother came out of the house carrying a

pail. She stood still, listening, wondering what was the matter.

The reeds made landing difficult. Maigret was in such a hurry that he sank up to the knee in the muddy water. James alighted with more dexterity and shambled after him, muttering to himself.

There was no need to ask the way. Everybody was trooping round to the back of the shed.

A man was standing there, looking at the others with large troubled eyes, repeating over and over again:

"It wasn't me. . . ."

The man was Basso. He hardly seemed conscious of what he was holding in his hand—a small revolver inlaid with mother-of-pearl.

"Where's my wife?" he asked, looking at those who stood round him as though he did not know them.

Heads were turned, looking for her. Then someone said:

"She stayed behind, to see to the dinner."

Maigret had to thread his way through to the front before catching sight of the figure that was lying in the tall grass, the figure of a man in a gray flannel suit, with a straw hat fallen on the ground beside him.

There was nothing tragic about it. On the contrary, it was all rather ridiculous. Nobody had the faintest idea what to do. All they did was to stand gaping at Basso, who gaped wildly back at them. What made it still more absurd was that the doctor was standing quite near the body, and he seemed just as nonplused as anybody. One might have thought he was waiting for instructions before daring to intervene.

Then the body moved. And suddenly the atmosphere changed, became tragic after all. A leg twitched. The shoulders squirmed. An effort—a desperate effort—then the body fell back limply on to the grass.

Monsieur Feinstein was dead.

"Feel his heart," said Maigret curtly to the doctor.

He was familiar with scenes of this sort, and his keyed-up senses missed no detail. His eye took in the whole scene with a sharpness of focus that made it almost unnatural.

In the last ranks of the spectators, someone had sunk to the ground, wailing piteously. It was Madame Feinstein, who had been the last to arrive, having been the last to stop dancing. Others were bending over her. The innkeeper appeared with the mistrustful, almost hostile look of a typical peasant.

Monsieur Basso was panting. His breast heaved. Suddenly, looking down, he noticed the revolver he was holding. At the sight of it he seemed more bewildered than ever. Once more he looked wildly at the people gathered round him, as though imploring one of them to be kind enough to take it from him. Or was he still looking for his wife? For the tenth time he repeated:

"It wasn't me."

"Dead," said the doctor, raising his head.

"A bullet?"

"It went in here."

And he pointed to a gap between the ribs.

"Is there a telephone here?"

"No," answered the landlord. "You have to go to the station or up to the lock."

Marcel Basso was in white flannels, and his open shirt made the most of his beefy chest. But his massive build was of no use to him now. He swayed slightly from side to side, stretched out a hand as though groping for support, then abruptly sat down on the grass, barely three yards from the corpse, and took his head between his hands.

"Poor man! He's crying!"

It was a little, high-pitched voice which piped up, somewhere in the rear. It was intended to be in an undertone, and the girl blushed scarlet as heads were turned in her direction.

"Have you got a bicycle?" Maigret asked the landlord.

"Of course."

"Then go to the lock as quick as you can. Tell the lock-keeper to ring up the *gendarmerie*. . . ."

"At Corbeil or Cesson?"

"Whichever he likes."

Maigret looked rather put out as he studied Basso, then picked up the little revolver that lay in the grass. One cartridge had been fired.

A lady's revolver, pretty as a piece of jewelry.

Tiny nickel-plated bullets. They didn't look serious at all. Yet one of them had been enough to snap the thread of a human life.

There was no blood to speak of. Just a little rusty-red spot on the gray flannel jacket, apart from which the hosier looked as spick and span as ever.

"We've taken Mado indoors," said a young man, rejoining the group. "She's in an awful state."

Mado was Madame Feinstein. She was at that moment lying on the innkeeper's high, old-fashioned, wooden bed. Everybody stared at Maigret, except those at whom he looked, who turned their eyes hurriedly away.

"Cooey! . . . Where are you all?"

The words, coming from the riverbank, cast a sudden chill. It was Pierrot, who had just arrived in his canoe to join them.

"Go quickly. . . . Go and stop him. . . ."

Monsieur Basso was recovering his self-control. He raised his head, ashamed of his momentary weakness. Once again he looked from face to face as though seeking someone who could help him.

"I belong to the *Police Judiciaire,*" said Maigret.

"You know. . . . It wasn't me. . . ."

"I'd like to have a word with you, if you'll come this way."

Then, turning to the doctor, the inspector went on:

"I count on you to see that nobody touches the body, or comes near it at all."

It was all rather flat, like a rehearsal in everyday clothes. There was no drama in this glowing, sultry air, with anglers passing to and fro along the towing-path, their creels slung across their backs. Maigret and Basso walked off side by side.

"It's incredible. . . ."

There was no spring left in Basso's stride. As soon as they turned the corner of the shed they could see the river, the villa standing on the other bank, and Madame Basso rearranging the wicker chairs that were lying about all over the garden.

Seeing his father, the boy called out:

"*Maman* sent me over to get the key of the cellar. . . ."

Monsieur Basso was unable to answer. His eyes changed to those of a hunted beast.

"Tell him where the key is."

With an immense effort Basso just managed to call out:

"It's hanging on the latch of the garage."

"What?"

So he had to say it over again:

"On the latch of the garage."

A faint echo came back to them:

". . . rage."

They went in under the lean-to and stood by the automatic piano.

"What happened between you?"

"I don't know. . . ."

"Whose is this revolver?"

"It's not mine. I always keep mine in the car."

"Did Feinstein attack you?"

A long sigh, followed by a long silence. Then:

"I don't know. . . . I didn't do anything. I swear I didn't kill him."

"But you had the revolver in your hand when . . ."

"Yes. . . . But I really don't know how it happened."

"Do you mean to say someone else shot him?"

"No . . . I . . . You've no idea how awful it is."

"Or did Feinstein shoot himself?"

"He . . ."

Monsieur Basso sat down on one of the benches and took his head between his hands. There were several glasses on the table, one of them no more than half-empty. He seized it, and with a grimace gulped down its contents.

"What's going to happen now? Are you arresting me?"

Wrinkling his forehead, he stared intently at Maigret and then went on:

"But . . . How is it you happened to be here? . . . You couldn't possibly have known . . ."

To judge by his distorted features, he was making a supreme effort to understand something, or rather to piece together a number of discordant scraps of thought.

"It almost looks . . . almost like a trap, which . . ."

The white canoe had crossed to the other side and was now returning.

"Papa! The key isn't there. *Maman says* . . ."

Mechanically Basso patted his pockets, from one of which came a metallic sound. He took out a bunch of keys, putting them on the table, and it was Maigret who walked over to the towing-path and called out to the boy:

"Here! Catch!"

"Merci, monsieur."

And once again the canoe shot over towards the other bank, where Madame Basso and a maid were laying the garden tables for dinner. Downstream, at the *Vieux Garçon,* boats were tying up for the night. The proprietor of the *Guinguette à Deux Sous* came pedaling back from the lock, where he'd been to telephone.

"You're sure it wasn't you who pulled the trigger?"

No answer. Basso merely shrugged his shoulders and heaved another sigh.

Pierrot had jumped ashore and run up to his mother. They talked together for a moment or two; then an order was given to the servant, who went into the house, returning almost immediately holding something in her hand.

She handed it to her mistress. Fieldglasses. Madame Basso trained them on the *Guinguette,* and gazed through them for a long time.

Meanwhile James was in the kitchen with the people of the inn, filling up glass after glass of cognac as he thoughtfully stroked the cat that was coiled up in his lap.

4

The Meetings at the "Taverne Royale"

It was a horrid week, filled with tiresome little jobs with nothing to show for them, time wasted, irksome enquiries. And all in a stuffy, sunbaked Paris, whose streets were turned into rivers by a thunderstorm which drenched the town about six each evening.

Madame Maigret was still away, writing . . . *the weather is magnificent, and I've never seen such a crop of sloes as we shall have this year. . . .*

Maigret hated Paris when his wife was not there. He ate without appetite at the first restaurant that came to hand, and he had even been known to spend the night at a hotel to avoid going home.

The case had begun with a flat-brimmed top-hat in a shop in the Boulevard Saint-Martin. Then a clandestine rendezvous and a flying visit to the Avenue Niel. A farcical "wedding" at the *Guinguette à Deux Sous;* a few rubbers of bridge; and lastly the unexpected calamity.

When the *gendarmes* had arrived on the scene; Maigret had left it all to them, since he wasn't there officially. They had promptly arrested the coal-merchant and reported the case to the examining magistrate.

An hour later, Marcel Basso was sitting between two sergeants in the little station at Seineport. A record Sunday crowd was gathering to catch the train. One of the sergeants offered him a cigarette.

The lamps had all been lit, and there was only a smudge of twilight in the west. The train was just coming into the station, and everybody was bracing himself to fight for a seat, when suddenly Basso, without the faintest warning, broke away from his escort, dived through the crowd, dashed across the line in front of the engine, and made for the woods that were only just on the other side.

The *gendarmes* were taken completely unawares. Ten seconds before, he had been sitting between them, quiet as a lamb and apparently completely overcome by the sudden disaster that had overtaken him.

Maigret only heard of it after his return to Paris the same evening. It was an unpleasant night for everybody. All round Morsang and Seineport, *gendarmes* were combing the countryside, keeping a watch on stations, and stopping every car on the road. The net was spread over practically the whole of the department, and Parisians returning from their Sunday outing were astonished at the number of police on duty at the gates of Paris.

Two men of the *Police Judiciaire* were stationed at the Bassos' house on the Quai d'Austerlitz, and another two at their villa on the Seine. Lastly, two were covering the Feinsteins' flat in the Boulevard des Batignolles.

On Monday morning the examining magistrate and a host of experts proceeded to the *Guinguette à Deux Sous*. Maigret had to attend. There were interminable discussions.

That night there was still no sign of Basso. And it seemed practically certain that he'd slipped through the net. He might be hiding in Paris or one of the outlying towns—Melun or Fontainebleau, for example—though he might easily have gone farther afield.

On Tuesday morning the police pathologist presented his report. The shot had been fired at a distance of about a foot. There was nothing to show whether it had been fired by Feinstein himself or by Basso.

Visit to the Feinsteins' flat. A commonplace interior, without luxury, and none too clean. They kept a servant, but the Feinsteins were obviously people in a small way.

Questioned about the revolver, Madame Feinstein said it was hers. She had no idea her husband had taken it. She had always kept it in her own room. It was always loaded.

And Madame Feinstein wept and wept, ever

more copiously. It was difficult to get any other response out of her except the phrase "If only I'd known . . ." which she volunteered incessantly.

She had been Basso's mistress for the past two months. She was in love with him.

"But you had others before him?"

"Monsieur!"

She certainly had, whatever she might say about it. *Une femme à tempérament*, who was not likely to be satisfied by any husband.

"How long have you been married?"

"Eight years."

"Did your husband know of your *affaire* with Basso?"

"Good gracious, no."

"But he might have had suspicions?"

"Never."

"Supposing he had, do you think he might have been capable of threatening to shoot Basso?"

"I don't know. . . . He was a strange man, very reserved."

Certainly a household where there was no intimacy. Feinstein buried in his own affairs. Mado rushing round the shops and carrying on with other men.

It was a gloomy Maigret who conducted the case, wearily following in the traditional rut, questioning the *concierge* at the Boulevard des Batignolles, the manager of Feinstein's shop, the Bassos' servants, anybody, in fact, who had anything to do with either household.

The case didn't taste nice. A musty taste of commonplace existence, with a remote undercurrent of something a bit crooked.

Feinstein had started with a very small shop in the Avenue de Clichy. Then, a year after his marriage, he had taken over a going concern in the Boulevard des Capucines.

The deal had been financed largely by an advance from his bank, and from then on it had been the same story as with nine out of ten businesses that have no solid backing. Creditors pressing all the time, wholesalers threatening to cut off supplies unless their claims were met. An anxious passage at the end of every month, when payments fell due.

Nothing dishonest. But nothing solid either.

At home it was the same; the local tradesmen constantly clamoring for their bills to be paid.

In the little office behind the shop, Maigret pored for a good two hours over the books. Search as he might, however, he could find no dealings that were in the least remarkable six years before. That was the time Lenoir had referred to when he'd talked to Maigret on the eve of his execution.

A dull case and a discouraging one. Nothing to get hold of. A blank drawn at every turn.

Maigret rather dreaded the inevitable visit to Madame Basso, who had remained in the country. But her attitude astonished him. She certainly suffered, but she was far from being overcome. Altogether, she showed a dignity that was quite unexpected.

"My husband must have had good reasons to break away from the police."

"Flight is generally taken as a sign of guilt."

"I'm confident of his innocence."

"Have you heard from him?"

"Not a word."

"How much money had he on him?"

"Not more than a hundred francs."

Basso's affairs were in a very different state to Feinstein's. The offices on the Quai d'Austerlitz showed every sign of prosperity. In good years and bad, the business had never brought in less than five hundred thousand francs. The three barges alongside the yard were his own. It had been a substantial business in his father's time, and Marcel Basso had considerably extended it.

Nor did the weather help to improve Maigret's temper. Like most stoutly built people, he suffered from the heat, and up to three o'clock each afternoon the sun beat mercilessly straight down into the breathless streets.

Even when the sun moved westwards it hardly improved matters, and relief only came with the evening storm. And what a relief! The sky would blacken. A sudden gust of wind would fill your mouth with grit. Then claps of thunder, and the deluge would begin. Huge drops splashing on the asphalt, torrents coursing along the gutter.

Everyone took shelter in doorways or under awnings—and some of the awnings made a poor show of doing their job.

It was on the Wednesday that Maigret, caught

in the storm, made a dash for the terrace of the *Taverne Royale*. A man rose from his seat, holding out his hand. It was James, at a table by himself, with a Pernod in front of him.

It was the first time the inspector had seen him in town clothes. They made him look much more ordinary, but, even so, there was something about him which differentiated him from the average bank clerk, and which in some queer way made you think of a circus.

"Have a drink?"

Maigret was tired out. Heaven knows how long the rain would last, and after that he had to go back again to the Quai des Orfèvres to see if anything fresh had come through.

"A Pernod?"

In the ordinary way, he confined himself to beer. This time, however, he didn't protest. Still plunged in gloom, he sipped at the imitation absinthe. All the same, James was not an uncongenial companion. Indeed, there was one thing about him that was a priceless blessing; he wasn't a chatterbox.

He just sat back serenely in his wicker chair, smoking cigarettes and watching the few people who ventured out into the rain.

When a newspaper boy came by with an evening paper, he beckoned him. After a cursory look, he handed it to Maigret, pointing to a small paragraph:

Marcel Basso, the murderer of the hosier of the Boulevard des Capucines, is still at large in spite of the intensive efforts of the Paris police and the country gendarmerie to locate his whereabouts.

"And what do you think about it?"

James shrugged his shoulders, and the vague movement of his hand might be taken to mean he didn't very much care.

"Do you think he might have left the country?"

"I don't suppose he's very far. Probably wandering about in Paris."

"Why do you say that?"

"I don't know. All I know is, that if he fled it was most likely for some special reason. . . . Waiter! Two Pernods."

They were potent, and Maigret drank three. Little by little he slipped into a condition that was rare to him. Not that he was drunk—but everything became a bit softened, a bit blurred.

An agreeable condition. His whole being relaxed. He found it nice to sit there with James on the terrace of the *Taverne Royale,* watching the heavy straight rain. His mind lazily turned over the case he was working on, and it was the first time he thought of it—yes, actually with a touch of pleasure.

A desultory conversation, yet one which never seemed to flag. They touched on one topic, then on another, with long silences in between. Sharp at eight, James stood up, saying:

"Time to go. My wife will be waiting for me."

When Maigret walked off, his ill-humor returned. He was annoyed with himself for having wasted two hours, and his head was rather heavy with the Pernods.

He dined at the first likely-looking restaurant, and then returned to his office. No news of any sort. Not the faintest trace of the missing man.

And the next day he went on with the job, with the same sullen obstinacy.

For the most part it consisted in wading through old files, dating five, six, or seven years back. No result. Nothing which appeared to have the remotest bearing on the story Jean Lenoir had told.

Was it any good trying to find the Victor the latter had mentioned—his tuberculous fellow-blackmailer? Maigret tried, ringing up one sanatorium after another.

Plenty of Victors. Too many! But never the right one.

By lunch-time Maigret had a headache and wasn't feeling like food at all. He went, nevertheless, to the restaurant in the Place Dauphine, whose customers were mostly drawn from police headquarters.

In the afternoon he rang through to the detectives who were covering the Bassos' villa by the Seine. They had nothing to report. Nobody had been seen coming or going except the local tradespeople. Madame Basso had been seen in the garden with her son. She took in a lot of newspapers, but otherwise there was nothing unusual about the household.

At five o'clock Maigret was leaving the block of bachelor apartments in the Avenue Niel, where he'd been on the offchance of gleaning some further information about Basso or Mado. Once again; results nil.

And without any set intention, more as if it was an old-established habit, Maigret drifted toward the *Taverne Royale,* shook the hand that was held out to him, and took his seat on the terrace by James's side.

"Any news?" asked the latter.

And then to the waiter:

"Two Pernods, please."

The thunderstorm was late today, and they sat gazing out on to a street flooded with sunshine. Cars drove past, many of them driven by foreigners.

"The line the papers are taking," muttered Maigret, as though speaking more to himself than his neighbor, "the line the papers are taking is that for some reason or other Feinstein attacked Basso, who snatched the revolver out of Feinstein's hand and shot him."

"Which, of course, is quite absurd."

Maigret looked at James, who also seemed to be soliloquizing.

"Why should it be absurd?"

"Because if Feinstein had wanted to shoot Basso he'd have done it. Didn't you see the way he played bridge? Not the man to bungle anything."

Maigret couldn't help smiling: James said it so seriously.

"So in your opinion . . . ?"

"Oh, no! I've no opinion at all, except that

Basso had no need to go messing about with Mado. . . . On the other hand, she's not the woman to let a man slip through her fingers."

"Was her husband jealous?"

"Feinstein?"

And as James shot a glance at the inspector there was an ironical twinkle in his eye. Then, with a shrug of his shoulders, he went on:

"It's no business of mine. But if he had been jealous, most of the male members of the gang would have been dead and buried long ago."

"So they all . . . ?"

"Not quite all. No need to exaggerate. But if you once got dancing with Mado it didn't stop at that."

"You too?"

"I don't dance."

"But a woman can't carry on like that without her husband finding out sooner or later."

It was with a sigh that James answered:

"Perhaps. But Feinstein owed money to them all."

Maigret whistled.

"So that's it!"

"Deux Pernods. . . . Deux."

He was a queer fish, this James. You might sum him up at sight, putting him down merely as an ass and an alcoholic. But you'd be wrong! There was more in him—a lot more—than met the eye.

"Yes. And I don't for a moment suppose Mado knew a thing about it. Feinstein had only to saunter up to her latest flame and ask for the loan of a few hundred francs. No need to be heavy-handed about it. A meaning look and a little pressure to fork out. It wouldn't be so easy to refuse."

The thunderstorm still held off. The conversation lapsed, and Maigret, sipping his Pernods, stared vacantly into the street at the crowd that flowed by. He was comfortable in his wicker chair as he lazily ruminated what James had told him.

"Eight o'clock. I must be going."

James shook hands and strolled off just as the first big drops of rain were falling.

By Friday, it really was an established habit, and Maigret went to the *Taverne Royale* as a simple matter of routine. In the course of a rambling conversation he couldn't help saying:

"So you never go straight home from the bank? From five to eight you . . ."

The Englishman sighed.

"One must have some place one can call one's own."

A place to call one's own! The terrace of a café. A wicker chair, a marble table, and on it an opalescent green drink. For horizon, the columns of the Madeleine, the ceaseless flow of cars and pedestrians, and the bustling to and fro of the white-aproned waiters.

"How long have you been married?"

"Eight years."

Maigret didn't dare ask him if he loved his wife. In any case, he felt sure he'd say yes. Only, if it was yes, it was after eight o'clock, after three hours of a place he could call his own.

Wasn't it something like intimacy that was springing up between these two men?

That day they didn't even refer to the case. Maigret drank his three Pernods, only too glad to forget all about his work. Two inspectors were away, and he had to keep an eye on their jobs as well as his own. And there wasn't a single interesting one among them—nothing but rather tiresome details. To make matters worse, the examining magistrate who was handling the *Guinguette* case never gave him a moment's peace. Only that day he had sent him to interview Mado for the second time. Everything, in fact, had to be done twice over. For the second time he had gone through the hosier's books, and at Basso's office he had asked all the questions he had asked before.

Being short-handed at the *Police Judiciaire*, they hadn't enough men to cover all the places where they thought Basso might turn up. That didn't improve matters either, and the director of the *Police Judiciaire* was in as bad a mood as Maigret.

"About time you got hold of something!" he'd said that morning.

Maigret agreed with James. He too felt that Basso must be in Paris. But how could he have provided himself with money? Or, if he hadn't any, how did he live? What was he hoping for, or waiting for? Was he hiding for some special reason, as James had suggested?

The case against him would have been by no means damning. With a tip-top lawyer he'd have stood an excellent chance of getting clean off, or at any rate of being let off lightly. A short term of imprisonment perhaps, after which he'd return to his fireside and his fortune.

Instead of that, he'd bolted and spoilt everything.

It certainly looked as though he must have special reasons.

Saturday brought a firmly worded telegram from Madame Maigret:

Counting on your coming this weekend without fail love.

Maigret hesitated, then let the afternoon trains slip by, intending to take the night one. Soon after five he was in his usual place by James's side, while a couple of Pernods stood on the table in front of them.

As on the previous Saturday, there was a general exodus from Paris. People hurrying towards the Gare Saint-Lazare. Taxis piled high with luggage.

"Are you going to Morsang?" asked Maigret.

"Same as usual."

"It'll seem queer without Basso, won't it?"

The inspector was dying to go too. On the other hand, he wanted to see his wife, spend a few hours' trout-fishing in the streams of Alsace, and sniff the good country-house smell he always associated with his sister-in-law's.

He turned it over in his mind. The pros and

cons were pretty well balanced. James got up and went inside the café.

There was nothing remarkable about that, and Maigret took no particular notice of either his departure or his return a few moments later.

Some minutes passed, five, perhaps ten. Then a waiter came up.

"Is either of you gentlemen Monsieur Maigret?"

"I am. What is it?"

"A telephone call for you, Monsieur."

Maigret went indoors and crossed the large room to where the telephone box was situated. He was frowning. For, in spite of the heat and the Pernods, he had his wits about him. And there was something fishy about this telephone call.

Before going into the box, he turned round towards the terrace. James was watching him.

"That's funny!" he muttered as he picked up the receiver. "Hello! Maigret speaking. . . . Hello! Who is it? . . . Hello!"

He was fuming with impatience by the time a girl's voice answered:

"What number do you want?"

"Who's that?"

"Operator. What number do you want?"

"But you rang me up, mademoiselle."

"You haven't been rung up from here. I've had no call for you in the last ten minutes."

In a flash Maigret had banged down the receiver, kicked open the door, and rushed back into the café. On the terrace, under the shadow of the awning, a man was standing talking to James. It was Marcel Basso, looking quite unlike himself in a mean suit of ready-made clothes that didn't fit him. His anxious eyes peered in towards the telephone box.

He saw Maigret at the same moment the latter saw him. His lips moved—a hasty sentence—and he had darted back into the crowded street.

"How many calls did you have?" asked the manageress at the cash desk.

But Maigret was outside before she had finished her sentence. The terrace was crowded. A waiter with a tray of drinks was blocking the way. By the time the inspector was on the pavement it was impossible to tell which way Basso had made off. Buses were going in both directions. Had he jumped on to one? Or into a taxi? There were dozens about.

With a scowl, Maigret returned to his seat. Without a word or a glance at James, he sat down. A waiter approached.

"The manageress told me to ask how many calls you had."

"*Zut!*"

Somehow Maigret knew James was grinning, and he rounded on him.

"I congratulate you!"

James inclined his head.

"How long did it take you and Basso to work out that little scheme?"

"All done on the spur of the moment. Two Pernods, waiter. And some cigarettes."

"What was he saying? What did he want?"

James leaned back in his chair and heaved a sigh, like a man who finds further conversation futile.

"Was it money? And where on earth did he get hold of that suit?"

"You'd hardly expect him to be walking about the streets of Paris in white flannels, would you?"

It was in white flannels that Basso had escaped. James forgot nothing.

"Is this the first time that you've got in touch with him?"

"That he's got in touch with me."

"And you've made up your mind not to talk."

"You'd do just the same, wouldn't you? I've been his guest a hundred times. I've nothing whatever against him."

"Was he wanting money?"

"He'd been watching us for half an hour. Yesterday I thought I saw him hovering about on the opposite pavement. But of course, with you sitting there, he didn't dare come across."

"So today you arranged for me to be called to the telephone?"

"He looked so tired."

"Did he have time to tell you anything?"

"Extraordinary how a suit of clothes can change a man!" sighed James, evading the question.

Maigret looked at him out of the corner of his eye.

"I suppose you know that by rights I could arrest you as an accomplice?"

"There are so many things that can be done by rights. To say nothing of the fact that rights aren't always so right as all that."

He spoke with the utmost simplicity.

"Waiter!" he called out, changing the subject. "Are those Pernods coming?"

"They won't be a moment."

"Are you going to join us again this weekend? The thing is that, with two to share it, it's well worth while taking a taxi. It's only a hundred francs or so, while by train . . ."

"And your wife?"

"Oh, she always takes a taxi. She shares one with her sister and two or three friends. With five of them, it works out at twenty francs a head."

"I see."

"You're not coming?"

"Yes. I'm coming. . . . Waiter! The bill, please."

"We'll each pay for our own, as usual."

They always did. So Maigret paid for his three, while James gave the waiter ten francs extra for the telephone job.

In the taxi he sat silent and preoccupied. It was not till they were passing Villejuif that he finally got it off his chest.

"I'm wondering where we'd better play bridge tomorrow."

It was time for the thunderstorm. The first big raindrops streaked the windows diagonally.

5

The Doctor's Car

One might reasonably have expected to find a changed atmosphere at Morsang. A week isn't long to live down such events as had occurred the previous Sunday. One of the gang was dead, another fleeing for his life.

Yet when Maigret and James arrived, the crowd they found gathered round a car was just the same as ever. All were in sporting rig save the doctor, who had not yet discarded his lounge-suit. It was his car they were standing round, a brand-new one that he had driven for the first time that day. They were asking questions about it, while he only too willingly expounded its merits.

"How many miles to the gallon did you say?"

Nearly all had cars of their own.

"Listen to the engine! You can hardly hear it ticking over."

The doctor's wife remained sitting in the car. She was enjoying the moment to the full. Her husband, Dr. Mertens, was about thirty. He was thin and unhealthy-looking, as dainty in his movements as a girl.

"Hello!" said James, barging through the crowd. "Got a new bus?"

With his loose-limbed stride, he walked right round it, eyeing it critically and muttering to himself. Then out loud:

"I'll have to try it out tomorrow morning! You don't mind, do you?"

How were they going to take Maigret's presence this time?

To all appearances, they didn't even notice he was there!

"Is your wife coming, James?"

"Yes, she'll be here presently. She's coming with Lili and the others."

Canoes were brought out of the garage and carried down to the water. Somebody was mending a fishing-rod with silk cord. Up to dinner-time, the gang was dispersed in various occupations, and during the meal there was not much general conversation, though now and again a few remarks would pass from table to table.

"Is Madame Basso here?"

"She's been here all the week. A rotten week it must have been for her!"

"What are we doing tomorrow?"

It wasn't long, however, before Maigret was made to feel that they could have done very well without him. No one openly avoided him, yet, unless James was with him, he found himself almost invariably alone, sitting on the terrace or wandering along the bank of the river. When night fell, he slipped away and went to see the men who were posted at the Bassos' villa. There were two of them, keeping watch throughout the twenty-four hours. They slept and had their meals in a little inn at Seineport.

"Anything doing?"

"Nothing whatever. *She* doesn't seem up to any tricks. We see her every day in the garden. The tradesmen come as usual; the baker at nine, the butcher a little later. Then a man comes round with vegetables about eleven. The milk's brought by a girl from a farm."

One of the ground-floor rooms was lit. They were apparently having supper late that day, for, through the thin check curtains, it was just possible to make out the boy, sitting with a napkin tied at the back of his neck.

The detective was keeping his watch in a little wood by the riverside.

"You know, it's simply swarming with rabbits here," he said regretfully. "If it wasn't for the job we could have a fine time."

On the opposite bank, the *Guinguette à Deux Sous,* where two couples were dancing. No doubt workmen from Corbeil with their girls.

* * *

The Sunday morning was like any other at Morsang, with fishermen stationed at intervals all along the riverbanks or sitting motionless in their green-painted boats moored head and stern in the stream.

A sailing-boat would pass every few minutes.

It all seemed so tranquil, so orderly, as though nothing untoward could ever happen to disturb it.

A pretty picture under a pure sky. Townsfolk peacefully enjoying a few hours' escape from city life. Was it a little too pretty, a little too peaceful? Perhaps. Something a little sickly about it, like an over-sweetened dish.

Maigret found James in a blue-and-white striped jersey, white trousers, and sandals, and an American sailor cap. For breakfast he was sipping a large glass of brandy-and-water.

"Slept well? *Tu as bien dormi?*"

He never said *tu* to Maigret when they were in Paris, but used the less intimate *vous*. But here he said *tu* to everybody, the inspector included. It would have been odd with anybody else, but not with James, who didn't even seem conscious of it.

"What are you doing this morning?" he went on.

"I think I'll trot round to the *Guinguette*."

"We'll all be there later on. We're having a drink there before lunch. Do you want a boat?"

"I think I'll walk, thanks."

Oh, no! He was given a pogo stick, which was the latest craze. He had never been on one before, and had a job to keep his balance. He was the only one in town clothes. When he reached the *Guinguette* it was only ten o'clock, and there wasn't a customer in the place.

At least so he thought, till he found a man in the kitchen eating a huge chunk of bread and a bit of sausage. The old grandmother was just saying to him:

"You must take care of yourself. I had a boy myself who refused to take any notice of it, and it made short work of him, though he was a big strong fellow—twice what you are."

Even as she spoke, the customer, with his mouth full, was seized by a fit of coughing. In the middle of it he caught sight of Maigret standing in the doorway. He frowned.

"Give me a bottle of beer, will you?" said the inspector.

"Wouldn't you be more comfortable outside? On a fine day like this. . . ."

No. He preferred to stay in the kitchen, with its deal table covered with knife-marks, its rush-seated chairs, and the huge pot that simmered on the hot plate.

"My son's over at Corbeil seeing about some soda water. They promised to send it over yesterday. . . . So if you wouldn't mind helping me to lift the trapdoor . . . ?"

A large trapdoor in the middle of the kitchen floor, through which came a raw, damp breath from the cellar. The bent old woman disappeared below, while the man went on eating, with his eyes fixed on the detective.

He was a young fellow of about twenty-five, pale and thin. He was fair; he hadn't shaved for some days; his eyes were very sunken, and his lips colorless.

What was most striking about him, however, was the way he was dressed and his whole attitude. He wasn't in rags; nor had he either the aloofness of the tramp or the insolence of the professional beggar.

He was a mixture, a mixture of shyness and self-assertiveness. He was at the same time humble and aggressive. One might almost say he was both clean and dirty. His clothes were really not bad at all, yet they must have been dragging along the road for weeks.

"Your papers!"

There was no need for Maigret to add:

"Police!"

For the fellow had understood right from the start. From his pocket he drew a filthy identity-card. Maigret read the name half-audibly:

"Victor Gaillard."

He quietly folded up the card again and returned it to its owner. The old woman emerged from the cellar and lowered the trapdoor.

"There you are," she said, opening the bottle; "you'll find that nice and cold."

Then she went back to the potatoes she had been peeling, while the two men quietly, almost casually, started their conversation.

"Last address?"

"The Municipal Sanatorium at Gien."

"When did you leave?"

"A month ago."

"Since when?"

"I've been broke. Wandering along. . . . You could pinch me for vagrancy, but they'd only have to put me back in a *sana*. I've only one lung left."

He wasn't pitiful about it at all. Oh, no! Much more like a man presenting his credentials.

"You got a letter from Lenoir, didn't you?"

"What Lenoir?"

"You can chuck that! He told you you'd find your bloke at the *Guinguette à Deux Sous.*"

"I'd had enough of the *sana.*"

"And had rosy visions of living at the expense of the friend you picked up by the Canal Saint-Martin. . . ."

The old woman listened uncomprehendingly, but without astonishment. It all sounded so natural. There was nothing to show that two men were fencing for all they were worth. A hen wandered in, pickering about under the table.

"What do you say to that?"

"I don't know what you mean."

"Lenoir talked."

"I don't know any Lenoir."

Maigret shrugged his shoulders, lit his pipe, and once more said:

"You can chuck that! You know as well as I do that I'll catch you at the first bend in the road."

"They can't do anything worse than a *sana.*"

"I know. We've already heard about your one lung."

Two boats rowed past, followed by a canoe.

"Lenoir wasn't leading you on. The chap's coming all right."

"It's no use. You won't get anything out of me."

"So much the worse for you. I'll give you till this evening. If you haven't come up to scratch by then I'll jail you for vagrancy. . . . After that, we'll see."

Maigret looked into his eyes, reading what was there as easily as a book. A type of man he knew all too well.

What a difference between him and Lenoir! They might have belonged to different races. Victor was essentially a hanger-on, the sort that is employed to watch for the police while others do the job, the sort that gets the smallest share in the pickings. The sort that is easily led into bad ways and has neither the character to make good nor to become a real crook. He had started at an early age hanging round doubtful places. With Lenoir he had had a stroke of luck, and for a time had probably lived quite well on the canal business.

Without his lung trouble, he would probably have been to the end on the outskirts of Lenoir's gang, being given an odd job from time to time. Instead, he had been sent to a sanatorium, where he was no doubt a thorn in the flesh of nurses and doctors alike, breaking rules, pinching things, making mischief. It wasn't hard to guess that he'd gone from punishment to punishment, from sanatorium to sanatorium, to finish up in some special home for delinquents that had been only too glad to see the last of him.

He wasn't frightened. For he always had that door of escape—his one lung. Obviously he was going to live on his lung trouble till the day he died of it. And Maigret was threatening to clap him in jail!

"Do you think I care?"

"So you refuse to tell me who he is?"

"Who?"

"The canal fellow."

"Don't know who you mean."

Yet his eyes twinkled as he spoke, and he picked up his hunk of bread and sausage, stuffed his mouth full, and masticated with obvious pleasure.

"Besides," he muttered, after swallowing at last, "Lenoir never blabbed. He wasn't the fellow to."

Maigret did not allow himself to be irritated. He'd got hold of the right end of the stick, or at least he'd got hold of something. It made the whole case look different now.

"I could do with another bottle, *grand'mère.*"

"I thought you might. I brought up three."

She looked with curiosity at Victor. She couldn't have failed to get the hang of their conversation, and she wondered what crime he could have committed.

"To think you were being taken care of in a *sana*—and you must needs go and leave. Just like my boy. He was just the same. Couldn't bear to be cooped up, as he used to say."

Maigret watched the boats passing in the blazing sun outside. The gang would soon be coming for their drink before lunch. The first to arrive were James's wife and two friends. As their boat came alongside, they waved to some others who were close behind. Still more were following.

Catching sight of them, the old woman sighed.

"There! And my son's not yet back from Corbeil. I'll never be able to manage all alone."

"What about your daughter?"

"She's gone for the milk."

All the same, she collected some glasses and carried them outside, placing them on the tables in the garden. Then she fumbled in a pocket of her petticoat.

"They'll be wanting some coins for the piano."

Maigret remained where he was, watching the gang arrive with one eye while keeping the other on his chesty acquaintance, who went on eating undismayed. And now and again his glance would fall on the Bassos' villa, with its garden full of flowers, the two boats moored up, the swing that hung from the branch of a tree.

He started, thinking he heard a shot in the distance. Others too seemed to have heard something. Heads were raised. People stood listening. But there was nothing to see, and for quite ten minutes nothing further happened.

The crowd that had come over from the *Vieux Garçon* took their seats at the tables. The old woman sallied forth with an armful of bottles.

Then a dark figure appeared at the Bassos' lawn, stopped for a moment, gazing at the *Guinguette,* then ran down to the water. Maigret recognized one of his men. It took him quite a time to cast off, then he rowed with all his might across the stream.

Maigret stood up, looking at Victor.

"You'll stay just where you are."

"Anything to oblige!"

Outside, nobody thought of ordering a drink. All eyes were turned on the man in black, rowing. Maigret walked down to the reeds by the waterside, where he waited impatiently.

"What's the matter?"

The detective was out of breath.

"Jump in. . . . I swear it wasn't my fault. . . ."

He rowed back, this time with Maigret in the stern-sheets.

"Everything was perfectly quiet. The man with the vegetables had just left. . . . Madame Basso and the boy were walking together in the garden. . . . I admit there was something funny about them. As though they were expecting something. . . . A car drove up, a brand-new one by the look of it, stopping exactly at the gate. A man got out. . . ."

"Rather bald, but still young?"

"Yes. Well, he joined the others, and the three of them walked up and down the garden, talking. . . . You know the place we watch from, don't you? Quite a little way off. Too far to hear anything that was said. . . . Then they shook hands, walked over to the car, and the chap got in and started her up. And just as he was putting the clutch in, the other two made a dive into the rear seats. . . . I hadn't time to get there. The car went off at the hell of a rate."

"Who fired the shot?"

"I did. I hoped to puncture one of the tires."

"Was Berger with you?"

"Yes. I was on duty, but he'd strolled over to have a chat. I sent him off at once to Seineport to telephone all round."

It was the second time the alarm had been given to all the *gendarmeries* of Seine-et-Oise. The boat had reached the other bank. Maigret jumped out and walked up the garden. What was to be done? Nothing. Only to telephone, and Berger was already doing that.

Maigret bent down and picked up a woman's handkerchief embroidered with Madame Basso's initials. It was wet and almost torn to ribbons by the chewing she had given it while waiting for James.

But what upset the inspector was the memory of all the Pernods he had drunk at the *Taverne Royale,* all those hours he had whiled away sitting lethargically by James's side, staring out into the sun-bathed or rain-drenched street.

He resented that memory, resented the thought that he had let himself slide, played himself false.

"Shall I still keep watch on the house?"

"What for? To see it doesn't run away too? . . . No, run over to Seineport as fast as you can. Take Berger with you and join in the hunt. See if you can get hold of a motorbike, so that you can keep me posted."

An envelope lay by the vegetables on the kitchen table. It was addressed to Madame Basso, and Maigret felt sure it was in James's writing.

The letter had evidently been delivered with the vegetables. It had told her to be ready. And from the moment she had received it she had walked nervously up and down the garden, her teeth tugging at the corners of her handkerchief.

Maigret walked down to the boat and rowed slowly back to the *Guinguette,* where he found half the gang clustered round Victor. Someone had stood him a drink, while the doctor was asking him questions.

And Victor was so pleased with himself that he actually winked at the inspector, as much as to say:

"Just you watch! I'm getting on beautifully."

Then he went on with his explanation:

"What they do—and it was a big specialist, or so they told me—what they do is to stick a hollow needle into you and blow you up like a tire. Then they stick the place up to keep the air in."

The doctor smiled at the crudeness of the description, but none the less nodded approval.

"They do it first on one side and then on the

other. You see, there's a lung on each side—isn't that right, Doctor?"

"Yet you drink stuff like that?"

"Oh, that much won't do me any harm."

"Do you have cold sweats at night?"

"Sometimes. Particularly when I sleep in a draughty barn!"

"What are you drinking, Inspector? I hope nothing's happened to make them send for you like that. . . ."

"Tell me, Doctor, is James using your car this morning?"

"He asked me to let him try it. He'll soon be back."

"I doubt it."

The doctor started, then tried to smile as he stammered:

"You . . . you're joking. . . ."

"There's no joke about it at all. He's using it at this moment to make off with Madame Basso and her son."

"James! . . ."

It was the Englishman's wife who spoke:

"James! . . . You don't mean . . . ?"

"Yes, I do. . . ."

"It must be a practical joke. He's always ready for anything of that kind."

The only one to enjoy himself was Victor, who kept his eyes on Maigret while blissfully sipping his *apéritif*.

The innkeeper returned from Corbeil in his pony-cart, filled with cases of siphons.

"More trouble!" he said as he passed the group. "You can't drive half a mile along the road without being stopped and questioned by a *gendarme*. Fortunately they all know me. . . ."

"On the Corbeil road?"

"Yes. They're at it now. At the bridge there's a queue of twenty or thirty cars. Everybody's got to show his papers. Everybody—not only the drivers."

Maigret looked away. It wasn't his doing. It was merely routine, and there was nothing else to be done. All the same, it was a coarse, clumsy method. No wonder people grumbled. It was a bit thick to be held up on the road two Sundays running. And not even for a sensational case. There had been too little to go on, and the papers hadn't treated it as front-page news.

But was it Maigret's fault, after all? Had he bungled the case? Once more his thoughts reverted to the *Taverne Royale,* to those hours spent sitting by James's side.

"What are you having?" he was asked again.

Maigret was fed up. Fed up with himself, fed up with everybody, fed up with the whole of this Sunday-at-Morsang atmosphere.

"Some beer," he grunted.

"At this time of the morning?"

And the well-meaning young man who had offered him an *apéritif* was astonished when Maigret let loose:

"Yes, some beer! And at this time of the morning!"

Victor, too, came in for a very nasty look.

Meanwhile the doctor was trying to forget about his car.

"An interesting case," he was saying to his neighbor, with a jerk of his head in Victor's direction. "They seem to have done the pneumothorax pretty thoroughly. . . ."

And then in an undertone:

"Not that it makes much difference. I'd give him a year at the outside."

Maigret lunched at the *Vieux Garçon*, sitting alone at his table, savage, ready to bite anyone who came too close. The second time Janvier came to report, it was to say:

"No luck. The car was sighted on the Fontainebleau road, but there's been no sign of it since."

The Fontainebleau road! Just the place! A fine jam there'd be, with literally hundreds of cars standing in queues!

Two hours later the news came through that a garage in Arpajon had supplied petrol to a car answering to the description that had been circulated.

But wasn't it a mistake? For the garageman swore there was nobody in the car except the driver.

It wasn't till five o'clock that a telephone call came through from Montlhéry to say the doctor's car had finally been located. It had been streaking round and round the racing-track, as though on a speed trial. Then one of the tires had gone flat and the car been brought to a standstill. It was more by luck than anything else that the policeman on duty there had asked to see James's driving license. He had been unable to produce one.

The garageman had been right. James was all alone. They asked Maigret what was to be done with him.

"Hold on," was the answer. "I'm coming."

"To behave like that with a new car!" whined the doctor. "I'm beginning to think the fellow's mad. Either that or he's drunk. . . ."

And he asked Maigret if he could come with him.

6

The Price for a Name

A car was procured, and Maigret drove off with the doctor. First of all, they went round to the *Guinguette à Deux Sous* to pick up Victor. The latter winked again—this time to the landlord as he took his seat. A wink which meant:

"Look what a fuss they're making of me!"

He sat facing Maigret. He even had the impudence to ask them to shut the window on account of his one lung.

There were no races that day on the track. A few people, however, were doing practice-runs in front of the empty pavilions. The lifelessness of the place made it seem all the vaster.

Some distance off, to one side of the track, was a car with a *gendarme* standing over it. Near it was a motorcycle whose owner, in a leather cap, was kneeling on the ground tinkering with the engine.

"There you are," said someone.

Victor was more interested in a racing-car that was haring round the track at well over a hundred miles an hour. Forgetting his lung, he eagerly opened the window to see it better.

"That's my car all right," said the doctor as they came to a halt. "Let's hope he hasn't ruined it."

Standing by the motorcycle, James was giving advice to the kneeling figure. He stood there with his chin in his hand, with apparently no thought for anything but the engine that wouldn't go, till suddenly, raising his eyes, he saw the others approaching.

"Hello! You here already?"

He looked Victor over from head to foot, apparently wondering what he was doing there.

"Who is he?"

If Maigret had set any store by this meeting, he was certainly disappointed. Victor, for his part, hardly looked at the Englishman at all. He was too interested in the racing-car. The doctor had opened the hood of his car and was ruefully wondering how much it had suffered by being driven like that before ever having been run in.

"Have you been here long?" growled the inspector.

"I really don't know. . . . Perhaps quite a time. . . ."

His self-possession was nothing short of incredible. No one could possibly have guessed from his manner that he had carried off a woman and a boy under the eyes of the police. No one could have guessed that it was on his account that the whole police force of Seine-et-Oise had been called out, and ten thousand cars stopped on the road.

"Don't worry," he said to the doctor. "There's no harm done except for the tire. I didn't really drive so fast. She's a nice bus. The clutch is a little stiff perhaps, but otherwise . . .

"I suppose that's what Basso came to see you about yesterday? Asked you to fetch the family?"

"You know very well, old chap, that I can't answer questions of that sort."

"Nor tell me where you took them?"

"Put yourself in my place. . . ."

"Well, there's one thing I give you full marks for. There aren't many professionals that would have thought of that."

James looked at him with modest surprise.

"What?"

"The racing-track. Having disposed of Madame Basso, you didn't want to be discovered too soon. The roads would soon be guarded, so you thought of this place. And if it hadn't been for the puncture you might still have been going round and round undisturbed."

"I always wanted to have a go at it one day, and it seemed a good opportunity. . . ."

But the inspector was no longer listening. He had caught sight of the doctor getting out the spare wheel.

"You can change the wheel if you like, but I'm afraid we'll have to keep the car."

"What? *My* car? What have *I* done?"

His protests were in vain. As soon as the wheels were changed, the car was put into a private lock-up and Maigret himself pocketed the key. James quietly smoked a cigarette. Victor still gazed at the cars that swished by. The *gendarme* asked for instructions.

"March this one off," said Maigret, pointing to Victor. "He's to be kept until further orders in a cell at the *Police Judiciaire.*"

"What about me?" asked James.

"Do you still refuse to tell me anything?"

"Put yourself in my place. . . ."

Maigret sulkily turned his back.

Monday was gray and raining. Maigret found it comforting, as it suited his own somber mood and the day's uncongenial tasks.

First of all, a report had to be written up on the previous day's events, a report in which the inspector was expected to justify the use he had made of the forces under his command.

At eleven he was called for by two experts of the *Identité Judiciaire* and driven down to the track at Montlhéry, where he stood around watching them at work.

The doctor had only driven forty miles since the car had been delivered from the works in the middle of the week. The total mileage now showing was just over a hundred and fifty. How much of that had been run on the track? From witnesses' accounts the evening before, it was estimated at about fifty. It was necessarily a rough estimate, but they had nothing else to go on, so it was assumed that James had driven about sixty miles before arriving at Montlhéry.

The distance by the shortest route from the Bassos' villa was barely twenty-five, so he had obviously been pretty far afield. A map was produced and a circle drawn on it to indicate his possible range of action.

Then came the examination of the tires with the aid of high-powered lenses. Dust and débris were carefully scraped out of the treads, and some was put aside for chemical or microscopical examination.

"Hello!" said one. "This looks like tar."

The map was referred to. It was a special map, furnished by the *Ponts-et-Chaussées,* showing all the work that was being done on the roads. Within the circle they had drawn there were five places, widely separated, where tar had recently been put down.

"Limestone dust. . . ."

Another map was produced, a military one, showing road surfaces. Maigret walked gloomily up and down, smoking.

"No limestone roads in the direction of Fontainebleau. But here's a stretch between Arpajon and La Ferté-Alais . . ."

A little later:

"Some grains of corn here. . . ."

The data gradually accumulated. The maps were heavily scored with red and blue pencil-marks. At two, one of them telephoned to the mayor of La Ferté-Alais to ask what building operations were going on in the town, and more precisely whether Portland cement was likely to have been spilt on any of the roads in the district. The answer didn't come through till three.

The water-mills on the Essonne were being reconstructed. There were traces of Portland cement on the road from La Ferté to Arpajon.

That was something, if not very much. The experts gathered up their instruments and specimens, and all three returned to Paris, Maigret to his office, the others to their laboratory.

For the best part of an hour, the inspector, with a map spread out before him, was telephoning through to country *gendarmeries* in the affected area.

With that done, he left his room, intending to have a chat with Victor, whom he had not seen since his arrest. But before he was halfway down the stairs an idea flashed across his mind. Hastily retracing his steps, he picked up the telephone and asked for the accountant in Basso's office.

"Hello! Police! Will you please tell me the name of your bank? . . . *Banque du Nord*, Boulevard Haussmann? Thanks. . . ."

He went straight there and asked for the manager. Five minutes later, another piece of data had been added to the case. At ten that very morning, James had entered the bank and cashed a check for three hundred thousand francs drawn by Marcel Basso.

The check was dated the previous Thursday.

"The chap downstairs wants to see you. Keeps on saying he's something important to tell you."

Maigret went ponderously down the stairs and entered the cell.

Victor Gaillard was sitting on a bench, his elbows on the table, his head on his hands.

"What is it?"

The prisoner jumped to his feet. A cunning look spread over his features. Shifting his weight from one leg to the other, he began evasively:

"You haven't found out anything, have you?"

"Go on! Cough it up!"

"You see! I knew you wouldn't. . . . I'm no bigger fool than the rest of you, and during the night I've been thinking things over. . . ."

"And you've decided to talk?"

"Just a moment! We must come to an understanding first. . . . I don't know what Lenoir told you, but I'm quite sure it wasn't very much. If he did talk, it wasn't enough to put you wise. In other words, without me you're stuck, and you'll go on being stuck. In fact, it'll only get worse and worse.

"No, you can't do without me, and what I says is this: a secret like that's worth money. A lot of money. After all, suppose I went to the fellow? What wouldn't he give me to keep my mouth shut? Anything I liked to ask."

Victor looked exceedingly pleased with himself, pleased as only those can be who are accustomed to be kicked and who suddenly find that the boot is on the other foot. All his life the police had treated him like dirt, and now he'd got the whip-hand. He grinned with satisfaction and did his best to look suitably important.

"It boils down to this: Why should I give a fellow away who's never done a thing to me? . . . And what can you do to me if I don't? You could have me jailed for vagrancy, I don't say you couldn't. Only, you'd be forgetting that lung of mine. After two days I'd be in the infirmary, and after two more they'd send me back to a *sana.*"

Maigret looked hard at him, but said nothing.

"Now, what'd you say to thirty thousand francs? You can't call that a lot of money. Not for a thing like that. And it's no more than just enough to let me have a decent time for a year or two—and that's all the doctors give me. . . . Besides, what's thirty thousand francs to the Government? . . ."

Maigret was still listening. It seemed to be going splendidly. Victor had hardly thought it would be as easy as all that. He was exultant. A fit of coughing interrupted him, bringing tears to his eyes, but you might have taken them for tears of triumph.

Wasn't he cunning? And didn't he hold all the cards?

"It's my last word. Thirty thousand, and I'll

spew up the whole story. You'll get your man, and what's more, you'll get a pat on the back for having been so smart. . . . Thirty thousand, or you won't get a word out of me. Not a word. You can do what you like with me—it won't do a bit of good. Just think—it's six years ago, and there were only two witnesses. Only Lenoir, who's now wearing a wooden overcoat, and yours truly, Victor Gaillard."

He grinned again at his own facetiousness.

"Is that all you've got to tell me?" asked Maigret, who hadn't moved a muscle from start to finish.

"You think it's too much?"

It wasn't what Maigret had said, but his imperturbable calmness, that brought a note of anxiety into Victor's voice. For the inspector's face was like a stone.

"You can't frighten me, you know."

Victor forced a little laugh.

"And I know the ropes. I know all the tricks of your trade. You could beat me up, for instance. But wouldn't you know all about it afterwards when the papers got hold of it? And wouldn't I see they did? Beating up a one-lunged man. . . !"

"Is that all?"

"I tell you once more; you can't do without me, and that's a fact. And what's thirty thousand francs for . . . ?"

"Is that all?"

"And don't go thinking I'll give the show

away. If you release me, I shan't go running round to the fellow. No, nor writing either, nor telephoning . . ."

The voice was no longer the same. An anxious, plaintive voice. All the same, he struggled on.

"In any case, I want a lawyer. You can't refuse. And I know as well as you do that you've no right to keep me more than twenty-four hours without a charge."

Maigret blew out a cloud of smoke, thrust his hands into his pockets, and turned on his heel. To the man outside he said:

"Shut him up again."

He was furious. Now that he had left the cell he had no need to conceal his feelings.

It was enough to make anybody wild. He had his witness in the hollow of his hand. Yet what could he do to the dirty little . . . ?

Blackmail. A new sort of blackmail. Blackmailing Maigret himself on the strength of that bloody lung of his.

Three times, four times in the course of that little interview, the inspector had been on the point of hitting out. But he'd held himself in.

Just as well he had. Beating up a one-lunged man! Victor had been quite right. The papers would have squeezed the last drop of juice out of it. There were some that would have written up two whole columns on that one little fact.

Legally Maigret hadn't a leg to stand on. Victor had lived all his life on petty theft and dirty work of every kind. But that didn't mean there was a single charge to be preferred against him.

Except vagrancy. A wretched charge at the best of times.

And even then . . . If he did get sentenced, what was the use of that? His lung would pull him through anything. And didn't Victor Gaillard know it?

So he calmly asked for thirty thousand francs. And he was quite right, too, when he said they couldn't detain him more than twenty-four hours without charging him.

"Let him go," said Maigret savagely. "Let him go tonight at one o'clock. And tell Lucas not to let him out of sight."

And Maigret left the Quai des Orfèvres, biting viciously on to the stem of his pipe.

Just one word from Victor, and the case would be over. Without that one word he might go on floundering forever.

"To the *Taverne Royale,*" he snapped, after hailing a passing taxi.

James wasn't there, and though Maigret waited till eight o'clock, he never showed up. The inspector went round to the bank where he worked, where the night-watchman said he'd left as usual, at five.

Maigret dined off a plate of choucroute, then telephoned to his office.

"Has Victor asked to see me again?"

"Yes. He says he's thought it over, and he's ready to come down to twenty-five thousand, but not a franc less."

"Is that all?"

"And he says, in his condition, he's entitled to have butter on his bread. Then he says the cell's not up to regulation temperature."

Maigret rang off and wandered along the Boulevards. As darkness fell, he hailed a taxi, ordering the driver to take him to James's flat in the Rue Championnet.

Huge as a barracks, the house consisted of modest flats, inhabited by clerks, commercial travelers, and small *rentiers*.

"Fourth floor on the left," said the *concierge*.

There was no elevator, and the inspector slowly climbed the four floors, receiving on each landing, through the front door, a hint of the life within—the crying of a baby . . . the tinkling of a piano. . . .

James's wife opened the door. She was wearing a rather beautiful dressing-gown of royal blue. One couldn't say she was expensively dressed, but there was nothing poor about it either.

"Do you want to speak to my husband?"

The hall was no bigger than a good-sized kitchen table. On the walls were photographs of sailing-boats, bathers, and young people dressed in flannels.

"It's for you, James."

She pushed open a door, and followed Maigret into the room, going back to her chair near the window and resuming her crochet.

The other flats in the house were doubtless furnished in the usual stodgy, old-fashioned style. Here, on the contrary, there was definitely a touch of modernism. It was even a little arty-crafty and amateurish.

Partitions made of plywood had been put up to provide recesses and break the monotonous rectangularity of an ordinary room. Shelves had been put up too, and painted in bright colors. Apart from that, the furniture was scanty.

A plain carpet, startlingly green. The lamps were shaded with imitation parchment.

It was gay and fresh, but there was at the same time something flimsy about it. You had the feeling it would be unwise to lean too heavily against the walls, and also that the paint was still wet.

Above all, you had the feeling, when James stood up, that the place was too small for him, that he'd been shut up in a pretty box, in which there was not enough room to move about in or air to breathe.

Through a half-open door on the right, a tiny bathroom was visible. Just big enough to hold a bath and give a few square feet of standing-room. As for the kitchen, it was no more than a cupboard with a little gas-cooker standing on a shelf.

James had been sitting in a small arm-chair with a cigarette between his lips. He had just put down a book. And Maigret had the feeling that there was no contact at all between these two people on whom he had suddenly intruded. He was sure of it.

James in his corner. His wife in hers. One reading, the other crocheting. The noise of trams and buses passing in the street.

That was all. No intimacy whatever.

James came forward, holding out his hand, smiling rather awkwardly, as though it embarrassed him to be found in such a place.

"Hello, Maigret! How are you?"

But his easy familiarity didn't sound quite the same in this little doll's house of a flat. It clashed with the bright green carpet and the modern ornaments that stood here and there on the shelves.

"All right, thanks."

"Sit down. I was just reading an English novel."

And his eyes said clearly:

"Don't take any notice. It isn't my fault. This isn't *my* place. . . ."

His wife watched the two men, though without stopping her crocheting.

"Is there anything to drink in the place, Marthe?"

"You know very well there isn't."

Then to Maigret:

"It's his fault. If I keep any liqueurs here, they're only empty bottles in a few days. He drinks quite enough without that."

"Look here, Maigret! Suppose we went out for one?"

But before the inspector could answer, James's face clouded as he looked at his wife, who must have been making urgent signs behind Maigret's back.

"It's just as you like. . . ."

He sighed, closed his book, fidgeted with a paperweight that lay on a low table.

The room was certainly small. Very small indeed to contain two completely separate lives.

On the one hand, a woman proud of her pretty little flat, doing the housework, crocheting, making her own clothes.

On the other, James, returning home punctually at a few minutes past eight every evening, eating in silence, then reading a book till it was time to go to bed on that divan heaped with multicolored cushions.

It was easier now to understand the *Taverne Royale*.

"One must have some place one can call one's own!"

Certainly there was nothing he could call his own here.

And Maigret answered:

"Yes. Let's go."

James gave a sigh of relief and made for the door.

"Just a moment while I put my shoes on."

He went into the next room, leaving the door open behind him. But his wife hardly lowered her voice to say:

"Never mind him. He's not quite like other people."

She counted her stitches:

"Seven, eight, nine. . . . Do you think he knows anything about Feinstein's death?"

"Where's the shoehorn?" growled James.

They could hear him rummaging recklessly in a cupboard. Marthe looked at Maigret: a glance which meant:

"You see what he's like."

James returned, looking once more too big for the room.

"I shan't be long," he said.

"I know what that means!"

James made Maigret a sign to hurry. He was terrified Marthe might say something to prevent their going.

In the house next door on the left there was a bar frequented by taxi-drivers.

"It'll do, won't it? It's the only one handy."

A murky light shone on the zinc counter. At the back of the room, four men were playing cards.

"Good evening, Monsieur James. Same as usual?"

The landlord had risen to his feet and was already uncorking the Pernod.

"What's yours?"

"The same."

With his elbows on the bar, James asked:

"Did you go to the *Taverne Royale?* . . . I thought you might. I couldn't manage it today."

"On account of the three hundred thousand francs, I suppose?"

James's face expressed neither surprise nor embarrassment.

"Put yourself in my place. Basso's been a good friend to me, and we've had many a binge together. Here's how!"

"I'll leave the bottle with you," said the landlord, who was in a hurry to return to his cards. He evidently knew James.

"Poor chap," went on the latter, "he hasn't had much luck. To fall into the arms of a woman like Mado! . . . By the way, have you seen her lately? She came to the bank this afternoon to ask me if I knew where Marcel was. Can you beat that? . . . As bad as that doctor whose car I borrowed. And we'd always been good friends too. And now—would you believe it?—he's rung me up to say he's very sorry but he'll have to claim damages. . . . Here's how!"

James had poured himself out a second glass.

"What do you think of my wife? She's nice, isn't she?"

7
Old Ulrich

There was one thing about James which Maigret found interesting to watch as they leant over the bar. As the Englishman drank, his eyes, instead of growing vague, as is the case with most people, became on the contrary progressively sharper, until they shone with an acuteness that was positively penetrating!

His hand never let go of his glass, except to take hold of the bottle. The voice, unlike the eyes, was hesitating and toneless. He didn't look at Maigret—in fact, he didn't seem to look at anything at all. He appeared to let go—to sink into the atmosphere around him.

The card-players exchanged a word or two from time to time. The zinc which covered the bar reflected the lights dully. When he opened his mouth, James spoke dully too:

"It's funny. . . . A man like you—strong, intelligent — and others too—detectives, policemen in uniform, magistrates, all sorts of people. . . . How many are there on the go, all told? As many as a hundred? I shouldn't be surprised—not if you count all the clerks at work behind the scenes, and the telephone operators, and all the rest. . . . Anyhow, let's call it a hundred. A hundred people working day after day, night after night, all because Feinstein was plugged. And with such a tiny bullet!"

For a moment he stared into Maigret's eyes, and the inspector was quite unable to tell whether he was jeering or speaking with intense seriousness.

"Is it really worth all that bother? . . . And all the time that wretched devil Basso is a hunted man. . . . Last week he was rich. He had an excellent business, a car, a country villa, a wife and a son. And now he can't even show his head out of the hole he's hiding in."

James shrugged his shoulders and looked round him disgustedly, or perhaps merely sadly. The drawl in his voice became more noticeable.

"And what do we find at the bottom of it all? . . . A woman like Mado. A woman who needs men. . . . And Basso goes and walks into the snare. I suppose there aren't many men who'd have refused, what with her looks and her vivacity. . . . You think there's no harm in it, at any rate only once. But then it's twice, and then it's a habit."

James gulped down a whole mouthful of Pernod, then spat on the floor.

"Idiotic, isn't it? Result—one dead, and a whole family ruined. And a whole machinery started up, with a hundred people to turn the wheels. . . ."

What made it the more impressive was that he spoke without violence. It was no outburst. The words came out gently, lazily, while his eyes moved dejectedly from one object to another.

"I'll trump that," said an exultant voice behind him.

"And then Feinstein! Spending his life running after money, trying desperately to stave off disaster. That's all his life was—one long nightmare of scraping through by the skin of his teeth, squeezing his wife's lovers when there was nowhere else to turn. . . . And now that he's dead . . ."

"Or been killed," put in Maigret dreamily.

"Don't you think it would be rather hard to say which of those two had more effectively killed the other?"

There was a sort of dull, toneless morbidness in James's words which made the atmosphere around them seem thicker and murkier than before.

"Yes. It's idiotic. I can see so well what happened. Feinstein in desperate need of cash. No doubt he's been stalking Basso from the moment of their arrival. Even when he looks so preposterous, dressed up as an old grandmother, he's thinking of the bills of exchange that have to be paid on the Monday. He watches Basso dancing with his wife, wondering what it's worth. Do you see? . . . The next day he gets his chance and tackles him. Basso, who's already been stung before, isn't having any. The other insists, whines about ruin and dishonor. Suicide would be better than that, so he whips out the revolver. . . .

"And all the time, of course, he's making it obvious that he's not by any means so blind as he looks. . . .

"Yes, I'd swear to it. . . . Something like that, anyhow, and all on a glorious Sunday afternoon by the river.

"And Basso tries to stop him. At all costs he wants to avoid a scandal. Isn't his own villa standing just on the other side of the water? So he snatches at the gun. . . .

"That's all. . . . All except for a tiny little bullet in Feinstein's guts."

James turned his head slowly and looked hard at the inspector.

"And now tell me: what the hell does it matter?"

This time he actually laughed. A laugh full of contempt.

"So there we are! One hundred people—or it might be only ninety—running backwards and forwards like ants, because someone's gone and poked the anthill! A colossal manhunt for the wretched Basso, while Mado hunts him too, though for other reasons. Your husband may be shot, but that's no excuse for losing a lover!"

Then to the proprietor:

"*Patron!* How much is that?"

"But Basso's situation has changed a bit"—it was Maigret who spoke— "since he now has three hundred thousand francs in his pocket."

James merely shrugged his shoulders, as though to repeat once more:

"And what the hell does it matter?"

Then he started off again:

"I've just remembered how it all began. I mean between Basso and Mado. It was a Sunday afternoon, and the gang were at the Bassos', a lot of them dancing in the garden. Marcel was with Mado. Then someone bumped into them, or they tripped over something. Anyhow, they fell headlong, and right in each other's arms. . . . Everybody laughed. Even Feinstein."

James was picking up his change. He hesitated, put a coin down again.

"Just one more glass, *patron.*"

He'd already had six, and yet he wasn't drunk. All the same, his head must have been heavy. He frowned, and ran his hand across his forehead.

"And I suppose you've got to go back to your Basso-chasing. . . ."

He sounded as though he genuinely pitied Maigret.

"Three wretched devils; a man, a woman, and a boy hounded and harassed, all because one fine day the man went to bed with Mado."

Was it his drawling voice? Was it his loose-limbed disdainful figure lolling over the counter? Whatever it was, Maigret was fascinated, one might even say obsessed, and it cost him a great effort to see the case from any other angle.

What the hell did it matter?

It wasn't so easy to answer.

"Well, well!" went on James with a sigh. "I'd better be going, or my wife may be putting a bullet in *my* guts. She's quite capable. Oh, dear! How silly it all is!"

He opened the door and lounged out into the ill-lit street. Looking into Maigret's eyes, he said:

"A funny trade!"

"Being a policeman?"

"Yes. And being a man. . . . Do you know, my wife will go right through my pockets to see how much I've spent—in other words, how much I've had to drink. . . . *Au revoir*. Shall I see you tomorrow at the *Taverne Royale?*"

And Maigret was left alone, the prey of an uneasiness that took a long time to lift. It was as though all his ideas and all his standards had been thrown into the melting pot. Even the street looked different, and the people who went by, and the tram. . . .

Yes, it all looked just like the anthill James had spoken of. An anthill in a state of upheaval! Merely because one ant was dead!

The inspector's mind ran back to the hosier's body lying in the long grass behind the *Guinguette à Deux Sous*. And the people clustering round, and the *gendarmes* on the roads, and the traffic jams because of all the cars they stopped. An anthill's upheaval!

"Curse that fellow!" muttered Maigret with an annoyance that was not untinged with affection.

He set his teeth and tried to shake his mind free of the picture of futility James had painted. But it was difficult to pick up his previous trains of thought. He couldn't even remember why he'd come to see James at all.

"I suppose we'd better try and find out where James took the three hundred thousand," he muttered without conviction.

And all the words succeeded in doing was to impose a vision on his mind. The three Bassos, father, mother, and son, cringing in their hide-out, quaking at every sound outside.

"Curse him!" he muttered again. "And he always manages to make me drink more than I want."

Maigret wasn't drunk, but neither was he quite so sober as he would have liked. He went to bed in a thoroughly bad temper. He tried hard to focus his mind on other things, but snatches of his conversation with James kept coming back to him.

"One must have some place one can call one's own."

It was not only "some place," but a whole world of his own, that he stared into like a crystal-gazer through the mists of his milky-green Pernods, a world he casually lounged through, indifferent to the hard realities of life. . . .

A world, rather, in which there were no hard realities. A dreamy, unsubstantial world in which nothing really mattered, in which the rush and scramble of humanity had no more meaning than the scurrying of ants. . . .

This joyless, effortless outlook was terribly infectious. It had eaten its way into Maigret's brain to such an extent that he dreamt of the three Bassos, hiding in a cellar, listening in terror to the ceaseless tramp of men over their heads.

When he got up next morning, he was more than ever conscious of his wife's absence. She was still in Alsace, and the morning's post brought a postcard from her.

We are starting to make the apricot jam, and hope you will soon be here to taste it.

He sat down heavily at his desk, whose pile of letters tottered over onto the floor. He grunted a "Come in!" to his clerk, who was knocking at the door.

"What is it, Jean?"

"Lucas rang up. He says: will you go round to the Rue des Blancs-Manteaux?"

"What number?"

"He didn't say. All he said was Rue des Blancs-Manteaux."

Maigret glanced hastily through the letters to make sure there was nothing urgent, then went to the Jewish quarter of which the Rue des Blancs-Manteaux was the principal street, housing secondhand dealers of every description, clustered under the shadow of the great national pawnshop, the *Mont-du-Piété.*

It was only half-past eight. The day's business had hardly begun. At the corner of the street he sighted Lucas, walking up and down, his hands in his pockets.

"Where is he?"

For it was Lucas who had been told off to keep track of Victor Gaillard after his release at one o'clock the previous night.

With a jerk of his chin, the detective indicated the figure of a man standing at a shop window.

"What's he doing there?"

"I've no idea. Last night he began by wandering about. Then he found a seat, and lay down and went to sleep. At five he was moved on by a policeman, and he came round here almost at once. Ever since then he's been strolling about, but always coming back to the same place and staring into that window with the obvious intention of arousing my curiosity."

Victor, who had noticed Maigret's arrival, now lounged off, whistling pertly. Coming to a doorstep, he sat down on it, like a man who has for the moment nothing better to do.

Maigret looked at the name over the shop window:

Hans Goldberg
Articles Bought and Sold
Bargains of Every Description,

while through the glass he could just make out the little man with a pointed beard who stood peering out into the street, wondering what was going on.

"Wait for me," said Maigret.

He crossed the street and entered the stuffy, smelly shop, that was chock-a-block with old clothes and a medley of articles of all kinds.

"What can I show you?" asked the man half-heartedly.

At the back of the shop was a glass-paneled door, and in the room behind a fat woman was visible washing the face of her three-year-old boy. A basin of water stood on the table by a pile of plates and a butter-dish.

"Police!" said Maigret.

"I thought as much."

"Do you know the fellow who's been wandering about outside for the last couple of hours?"

"The thin one who keeps coughing? . . . I've never seen him before. I was bothered about his hanging about like that, so I called my wife, and she didn't recognize him either. . . . He's not one of us."

"And this man?"

Maigret held out a photograph of Marcel Basso, which the other studied attentively.

"He's not a Jew either."

"Or this one?"

It was Feinstein.

"Yes."

"You know him?"

"No, I don't know him. But he's one of us."

"You've never met him?"

"Never. We hardly ever go out."

His wife kept looking at them through the glass-paneled door. She had now taken her second baby from its cradle. It sent up a pitiful wail as the washing began.

The secondhand dealer seemed pretty sure of himself. He slowly rubbed his hands together, waiting for further questions, and he looked round him with the obvious satisfaction of a respectable tradesman who has nothing on his conscience.

"Have you had this shop long?"

"Rather more than five years. Long enough to build up a good business with honest trade."

"And before that, who had the place?"

"Don't you know? Old Ulrich, the fellow who disappeared."

The inspector heaved a sigh of satisfaction. This looked promising.

"Was Old Ulrich in the same line of business?"

"The police ought to know more about him than I do. All I've heard is that he didn't confine himself to buying and selling."

"A moneylender?"

"That's what they say. It seems he lived all alone. Nobody to do his housework. Nobody to help him with the shop. Then one day he disappeared, and the place remained shut up for six months. After that, I took it on, and if you make enquiries you'll find I've given it a different sort of reputation altogether."

"So you never knew Old Ulrich?"

"No. I didn't live in Paris in his time. Before coming here we were in Alsace."

The baby was still howling in the kitchen, while the elder brother had opened the door and was standing gravely sucking his finger as he stared at Maigret.

"That's all I know. If I knew any more, I'd willingly tell you."

"Right! Thanks."

After a final glance round him, Maigret went back into the street, walking up to Victor, who was still sitting on his doorstep.

"So you wanted to bring me here?"

"Where?" asked Victor, with obviously feigned innocence.

"What's this story of Old Ulrich?"

"Old Ulrich?"

"That's enough of playing the fool!"

"Never heard of Old Ulrich. I swear I haven't."

"I suppose he's the bloke who dived into the Canal Saint-Martin?"

"I've no idea. . . ."

Maigret shrugged his shoulders and walked off, saying to Lucas as he passed:

"Just as well to keep an eye on him still."

Half an hour later he was absorbed in the study of dusty old files. In the end he came upon the document he was seeking:

Jacob Ephraim Levy, alias Ulrich, aged 62, formerly of Upper Silesia, now secondhand dealer in the Rue des Blancs-Manteaux. Suspected of habitually infringing the usury laws.

Disappearance reported March 22nd. Had not been seen since the 19th.

No clues found in the house. No sign of robbery. 40,000 francs found sewn in mattress.

As far as can be ascertained, Ulrich went out on the evening of the 19th, a thing he frequently did.

No indications of his private life. Enquiries made in Paris and the provinces. No sign of him anywhere. Police in Upper Silesia informed, and a month later a sister arrived who took possession of all property after duly waiting till six months from date of disappearance.

At twelve o'clock Maigret was sitting in the district *commissariat* of La Villette. It was the third he had been to that morning, and he had had about enough of files. This time, however, the search was not in vain.

Taking a sheet of paper, he copied out:

July 1st. A body found by bargees near the lock in the Canal Saint-Martin. Taken to the Institut Médico-légal, *who report as follows:*

Male. Height 5 ft. 8 in. Apparent age between 60 and 65. Body in an advanced stage of decomposition. Clothing has been largely torn away. Nothing found in trouser-pockets. No ring or other distinguishing marks.

Maigret sighed with satisfaction as he returned the file to its shelf. At last he was clear of the vague and morbid atmosphere that James had been pleased to cast over the case.

He was now on solid ground.

There was no doubt whatever—at any rate, not to his mind. It was Old Ulrich who had been killed six years ago and thrown into the canal.

Why? Who had done it?

He smiled. That was what he was going to find out.

Bidding good-morning to his colleagues of the local *commissariat*, he went out into the street, where he slowly and voluptuously lit his pipe, standing all square on his heavy legs.

8

In Mado's Flat

The accountancy expert came into Maigret's office, rubbing his hands, his face wreathed in smiles.

"That's that!"

"What's that?"

"I've been right through the hosier's books again. Feinstein didn't keep them himself, but had a man in once or twice a week—a bank clerk, or something of the sort, who came round after hours. Everything quite straightforward apart from the usual little tricks to fool the tax-collector. The sort of business you can take in at a glance. And a business that wouldn't have been worse than hundreds of others if it hadn't been for lack of capital. Wholesalers were paid on the 4th or the 10th of each month. Always a struggle. Often bills were redated. Every now and again there'd be a sale to rake in a bit of cash at all costs. And then—Ulrich."

Maigret let him run on. He knew this voluble little man, who paced up and down the room.

"The same old story! . . . It's in the books of seven years back that Ulrich's name first appears. A loan of two thousand francs to be repaid on a certain date. It's no sooner paid back than it's borrowed again. And this time repayment is followed by a loan of five thousand. You follow? . . . Feinstein had found an unfailing source to tide him over difficulties. It becomes a habit. Six months later the initial two thousand has grown to eighteen thousand. And the loan of eighteen has to be repaid by twenty-five thousand. Old Ulrich isn't the man to do the job by halves!

"Feinstein struggles on. He always pays up on the nail, but only at the cost of getting deeper and deeper into debt. The twenty-five thousand are paid on the 15th of the month, and on the 20th another eighteen are borrowed. A few days after they're paid off, there's a fresh loan of twenty-five thousand. In the middle of March there's over thirty-three thousand owing."

"What happened then?"

"From that moment there's no further trace of Ulrich in the books."

Naturally! There was no trace of him anywhere! Except at the bottom of a canal! . . .

So Feinstein was thirty-three thousand francs the richer by the old moneylender's death.

"Who took Ulrich's place?"

"For a time nobody. The old man's disappearance must have given the hosier a breathing-space. It wasn't till a year later that he was in a tight corner once again and went to a small bank for credit. They gave it him, but they seem to have got tired of him pretty quickly."

"And Basso?"

"His name doesn't figure in the books at all. But Feinstein had been overdrawing his account in recent months, and I've found out from the bank that it was on the strength of a guarantee."

"Given by Basso?"

"Yes."

"And what was the position at the time of Feinstein's death?"

"Much the same as ever. The overdraft was never very much less. On the whole, it was mounting up slightly. . . . I dare say there are a thousand shopkeepers in Paris in much the same predicament, going through a small crisis every month when debts fall due, and just staving off bankruptcy."

Maigret stood up and reached for his hat.

"Thank you, Monsieur Fleuret."

"Would you like me to go into it further?"

"Not for the moment, thanks."

Everything was going well. The machinery James had scoffed at was turning round smoothly. Maigret, on the other hand, looked definitely glum, as though he mistrusted this very smoothness.

"Any news of Lucas?" he enquired of his clerk.

"He telephoned a little while ago. Victor's been round to the Salvation Army and asked for a bed. He's sleeping now."

That was not surprising, since he hadn't so much as a sou in his pocket. Was he still hoping to rake in thirty thousand francs by giving the name of Old Ulrich's murderer? Or rather twenty-five thousand, which he'd given as his lowest figure!

Maigret walked along the quays. Passing a post office, he hesitated, then went in. Snatching up a telegraph form, he wrote:

Probably arriving Thursday. Love to all.

It was Tuesday. He was still hoping to rejoin his wife before she returned from Alsace. He left the post office, filling his pipe as he went. Once again he hesitated, then hailed a passing taxi, giving the address of the Feinsteins' flat in the Boulevard des Batignolles.

He had handled hundreds of cases in the course of his career, and he knew very well that the great majority of them could be divided into two distinct phases.

The first consisted in the detective's making contact with a new atmosphere, with people of whose existence he had been unaware a few hours before, people who made a little world of their own, and whose little world had been suddenly shaken by the irruption of some drama.

Enter the detective, a stranger if not an enemy, encountering hostile or suspicious glances on every hand. Sullen faces, cunning faces. Or, on the other hand, the distraught faces of those who are racked by suffering or terror and have cast away the last shreds of reticence and self-respect.

This of course was the fascinating phase, at least for Maigret. The groping, probing phase, often without any real point of departure. A dozen different ways look equally hopeful—or hopeless. A dozen different people, and any one of them may be guilty, or at any rate an accomplice. Nothing to be done about it. Only to wait, to turn round and round, keeping one's nose to the ground. . . .

And then suddenly a scent is picked up. Something real, something definite. And with that the second phase begins. The clutch is slipped in, the machinery starts turning, and the investigation proper, relentless and methodical, begins. Each step brings fresh facts to light. The detective is no longer alone with his problem. Others are there too, hosts of others, and time is now on his side.

Even when there is no longer any doubt, the machinery goes on turning just the same, till everything is proved up to the hilt.

Only occasionally the vagueness and mystery of the first phase would last right up to the solution of the mystery. But those were the rare and marvelous exceptions. Those were the real Maigret "cases."

Where was he now? Maigret knew that the

body in the canal was that of Old Ulrich the usurer. And he knew that Feinstein had owed him money. Did that mean that the second phase had begun?

A quarter of an hour later he was knocking on the door of a fifth-floor flat of a house in the Boulevard des Batignolles. It was opened by a stupid-looking servant with straggling hair, who seemed uncertain whether to admit him or not.

But, looking over her shoulder, the inspector noticed something: James's hat hanging in the hall.

Was this indeed the second phase, in which everything moved forward with mechanical regularity?

Or was there a tooth broken on one of the wheels?

"Is Madame Feinstein in?"

By all appearances, the maid was new to the job and fresh from the country. Maigret took advantage of her awkwardness, and walked straight past her, making for a door behind which were voices. He had the grace to knock, but he opened it without waiting for an answer.

He knew the room already, not that there was very much to know it by. A little salon, just like ten thousand others, with its silly little armchairs with gilt feet. The first person he saw was James, who stood by the window, staring out into the street.

Madame Feinstein was dressed, all in black,

ready to go out, with a saucy little crêpe hat on her head. She appeared to be thoroughly worked up about something.

On the other hand, she didn't seem the least put out by the sight of Maigret. It was otherwise with James, whose face when he turned showed annoyance not altogether free from embarrassment.

"Come in, Inspector! . . . You've come at a very good moment. I was just telling James not to be so stupid. . . ."

"Ah!"

It looked exactly as though Maigret had butted in on a domestic squabble. It was in a hopeless, halfhearted voice that James pleaded:

"Look here, Mado . . ."

"Don't interrupt me. I was speaking to the inspector. . . ."

With an air of resignation, the Englishman turned back to his window to gaze at the foreshortened figures in the street far below.

"Of course, if you were an ordinary policeman, monsieur, I wouldn't think of talking to you like this. But you've joined in with the gang at Morsang. And, anyhow, it's not hard to see that you're the sort of man who's capable of understanding. . . ."

And she the sort of woman capable of talking for hours at a stretch! Capable of calling the whole world to witness on her behalf! Capable of silencing the most loquacious!

Really her good looks did not amount to very much. But there was certainly a freshness and sparkle about her that her black clothes showed up to all the greater advantage.

Obviously she'd be good fun, so long as it was only a question of fun. Just the sort to have a riotous affair with.

Impossible to imagine a more complete contrast to James, the loose-limbed, contemplative, phlegmatic James, who had not an ounce of crispness in the whole of his make-up.

"Of course, everybody knows that I'm Basso's mistress. And I'm not ashamed of it either. I've never made a secret of it. And there's not one of the crowd at Morsang who'd think of blaming me for it. . . . Now, if my husband had been another sort of man . . ."

She hardly paused for breath.

"After all, it's a man's job to support a woman, isn't it? And you can't keep a woman on debts. Just look at the place—look at the way I've had to live! . . . Besides, he was never here. Or, if he did spend an evening at home once in a way, it was only to talk of socks and shirts and braces, and his money worries, and the trouble he was having over one of the shop-girls. . . . And to my mind, if a man doesn't know how to make a decent life for his wife, he's nothing to say about it if she goes her own way. . . .

"Besides, Marcel and I were going to be married sooner or later. And that makes all the difference, doesn't it? You didn't know? Well, it isn't exactly the sort of thing one shouts from the house-tops. . . . It was only the thought of his son that made him hesitate. Otherwise he'd have been seeing about a divorce already. And so should I, and . . .

"Of course you know his wife, so you can judge for yourself. Not at all the sort of woman for him."

James sighed and sighed again. He was now staring at the carpet.

"And the question is: what is my duty now? Marcel's got in a mess, and of course the only thing is for him to go abroad. And obviously my place is by his side. Don't you think so? Tell me frankly. . . ."

"Hum! . . . Well! . . ." grunted Maigret, taking care not to commit himself.

"There you are, James! You see! . . . The inspector thinks just as I do. . . . Never mind about the world—I don't care what people say. . . . And this is the point, Inspector: James here is refusing to tell me where Marcel is.

"I can tell he knows by the way he talks. . . . You can't deny it, can you, James?"

If Maigret had not already had dealings with this type of woman, he would probably have been completely suffocated. But he no longer allowed himself to be taken aback by feminine inconsistency.

It was less than two weeks since Feinstein had been killed, apparently by Basso.

And there in the dismal little flat, with the hosier's photograph hanging on the wall and the hosier's cigarette-holder lying in an ashtray, his wife was talking of "her duty."

James's face was a picture! And not only his face. His shoulders, his whole attitude, the hang of his head—everything about him said:

"What a woman!"

She turned towards him.

"You see! The inspector . . ."

"The inspector has said nothing at all."

"There you go again! You simply disgust me. You're not a man at all—you're frightened of the least thing. . . . Supposing I were to tell the inspector why you came here today?"

It was so unexpected that James started. When he raised his head, his face had gone red as a beetroot. He was blushing right to the ears.

He wanted to say something. But he simply couldn't. He tried hard to recover his composure, but all he could produce was a painfully hollow laugh. Then at last he managed to say:

"Go on! Now you've started, you'd better tell him the whole story."

Maigret looked at Mado. She was a little disconcerted by what she had said.

"I didn't mean . . ."

"Oh, no! Of course you 'didn't mean.' That doesn't alter the fact that . . ."

The room seemed even smaller than before. Mado shrugged her shoulders in a way that meant:

"All right, I will. And so much the worse for you."

Maigret could hardly keep a straight face, so great was the contrast between the James he had known hitherto and the one that was now standing before him who lamely said, in answer to the inspector's inquiring look:

"Oh, well! I suppose you'd have found out sooner or later. . . . I've been with Mado too."

"Not for long, I'm glad to say," sneered Mado in return.

James winced at this answer. His eyes sought Maigret's as though for support.

"That's all. . . . It was a long time ago. . . . My wife never knew anything about it."

"And wouldn't she give you hell, if she ever did!"

"If I know anything about her, there'd be reproaches for the rest of our lives. . . . So I came to Mado to ask her to keep quiet about it, in case she was questioned."

"Did she promise?"

"On condition I gave her Basso's present address. Can you beat that? Especially as he's with his wife and his child. . . . In any case, I've no doubt he's across the frontier by now. . . ."

The voice failed ever so slightly at the last sentence. Obviously James was lying conscientiously.

Maigret had sat down in one of the little armchairs that creaked beneath his weight.

"So you weren't together very long?" he enquired in a good-natured, almost paternal tone.

"Quite long enough!" snapped Mado.

"No. Not very long," sighed James. "Only a few months."

"And I suppose you used to meet in a furnished room like those of the Avenue Niel?"

"James rented one in Passy."

"Were you already going to Morsang at that time?"

"Yes."

"And Basso too?"

"Yes. The gang hasn't changed much during the last seven or eight years. A few joining, a few leaving, but the bulk of them always the same."

"Did Basso know about you too?"

It was Mado who answered:

"Yes. He didn't take any interest in me then. It's only this last year that he's been in love with me."

In spite of himself, Maigret was beaming with satisfaction. He looked round the commonplace little drawing room with its ornaments, all of them more or less horrors. He mentally compared it with James's home, more ambitious, more modern, even rather studio-like.

And then Morsang and the *Vieux Garçon*, the rowing-and sailing-boats, rounds of drinks on the shady terrace in the midst of a landscape of almost unnatural prettiness.

For seven or eight years the same little crowd had been gathering every Sunday, boating and bathing together, drinking together, playing bridge in the afternoon or dancing to gramophone records.

But in the early days it was James who slipped

off behind the trees with Mado. And no doubt it was James who was the victim of Feinstein's equivocal glances as the latter asked for a small loan.

Everybody knew of Mado's affairs, except, as a rule, those most nearly concerned. Everybody conspired to keep what they knew from those who mustn't know: Basso no less than the others—until one day it was his turn to fall for her.

And now, in the Feinsteins' drawing room, it was a piquant little comedy that was being played out, what with Mado's brazen self-assurance and James's hangdog looks. Turning to Mado, Maigret asked:

"How long is it since you and James were washed up?"

"Wait a moment! It must be five . . . no, more than that . . . something like six years."

"How did it end? Which of you broke it off?"

James wanted to speak, but she cut in first.

"Both of us. We simply came to the conclusion we weren't meant for one another. In spite of his bohemian airs, James is a thorough *petit bourgeois* at heart. Even stodgier than my husband."

"But you remained on friendly terms?"

"Why not? The fact that you're no longer in love is no reason for . . ."

"Tell me this, James: at that time did you ever come to lend Feinstein money?"

"Me? . . ."

And before he could say any more, Mado had chipped in again.

"What do you mean? James lend money to my husband? Why should he?"

"Never mind! Just an idea that flashed through my mind. . . . All the same, Basso did."

"That's different. For one thing, Basso's a rich man. My husband used to get into difficulties—temporary difficulties. And he even spoke of having to leave the country and go to America. And to avoid that, Basso did, once or twice . . ."

"Yes, yes. I quite understand. But mightn't your husband have threatened to go to America six years ago?"

"What are you insinuating?"

She was all ready for an outburst of indignation. And rather than face a scene of outraged virtue, Maigret preferred to change the subject.

"I'm sorry. Perhaps I was saying more than I meant. Please don't think I was insinuating anything at all. . . . As for you and your affairs, that's your business. And nobody else's. That's what a friend of your husband's said to me once—a man called Ulrich. . . ."

With half-closed eyes he watched them both. Mado looked back at him with genuine astonishment.

"A friend of my husband's?"

"Or he may have been only a business acquaintance."

"That's more likely. For I've never heard that name before. . . . What was it he said about me?"

"Nothing. We were speaking of men and women in general."

James looked astonished too, but not quite in the same way. More like a man who smells a rat, and wonders what the other fellow's up to.

"That's all very well. But it doesn't alter the fact that James knows where Marcel is. And he refuses to tell me. . . . All right! I'll find out for myself. You see if I don't! . . . Though, as a matter of fact, it's more than likely he'll write to me to ask me to come. After all, he can't live without me."

James gave Maigret a look, an ironical look certainly, but still more a mournful one, a look that seemed to say:

Is it likely he'd want to have her on his hands again? . . . A woman like that! . . .

In a final attempt, she rounded on him once more.

"Well, James? Is that your last word? So that's all the thanks I get for all I've done for you!"

"You've done a lot for him?" asked Maigret.

"But . . . He was the first man for whom I broke my marriage vows. Is that nothing? I never thought of such a thing till he came on the scene. . . . Of course, he was different then. He dressed properly, and he still had a head of hair."

This was a case that had from the start seemed destined to alternate between the tragic and the farcical. Just now, farce held the floor so completely that it needed an effort to grasp the fact that a certain Ulrich had been done to death and his body shoved unceremoniously into a canal. And that, six years later, Feinstein had been shot behind the *Guinguette à Deux Sous,* as a result of which Marcel Basso and all his family were being hunted day and night by the police.

"Do you think he has a chance of crossing the frontier, Inspector?"

"I . . . I really can't say."

"If it came to that, you'd help him, wouldn't you? I'm sure you would. You've been a guest in his house. And you know the kind of man he is. . . ."

"I must be going," said James, looking all round the room for his hat. "It's high time I was back at the bank."

"I'll come with you," said Maigret hurriedly.

Anything rather than to be left alone with Madame Feinstein.

"Really? Must you?"

She would have liked to keep him.

"Yes. I'm afraid I must. We're shorthanded at headquarters. I'll come back another time."

"Marcel will be very grateful. And he's the sort of man who always repays a good turn."

She was very proud of her diplomacy. She could see it all perfectly—Maigret leading Basso by the hand up to the frontier, and gratefully pocketing a few bank-notes as a recompense.

When he held out his hand she gave it a long, significant squeeze. With a jerk of her head in James's direction, she whispered:

"We mustn't be too hard on him. . . . Since he's taken to drink, he's not quite what he used to be."

The two men walked down the Boulevard des

Batignolles without saying a word, James with his long swinging stride, staring at the ground in front of him, Maigret puffing away merrily at his pipe and seeming to enjoy the spectacle of the busy, crowded street.

It wasn't till they came to the corner of the Boulevard Malesherbes that the inspector asked casually, as though it was of no importance:

"Is it true that Feinstein never tried to get money out of you?"

James shrugged his shoulders.

"He knew very well that I'd none to lend."

"Were you already at the bank in the Place Vendôme?"

"No. I was doing commercial translation for an American petroleum company—I was earning barely a thousand francs a month."

"You had a car?"

"The Underground . . . and that's all I have for a car today."

"Were you living in the same flat?"

"We hadn't a flat at all. Only a bedroom in a cheap hotel."

He looked thoroughly bored. There was an expression of disgust at the corners of his mouth.

"Shall we have a drink?"

And without waiting for an answer, he dived into the bar they were passing and ordered two brandies-and-water.

"As far as I'm concerned, I don't care two hoots, but I don't see the point of bothering my wife. She's got enough to worry about as it is. . . ."

"Is her health bad?"

Another shrug of the shoulders.

"You don't imagine it's much fun for her, do you? . . . Apart from Morsang, where she does manage to amuse herself a bit. . . ."

He threw a ten-franc note on to the bar, then asked abruptly:

"Are you coming to the *Taverne Royale* this evening?"

"I might."

As he shook Maigret's hand he hesitated, then, looking away, murmured:

"About Basso. . . . You haven't found out anything, have you?"

"Professional secret!" answered Maigret with a kindly smile. "You're fond of him, aren't you?"

But James was already striding away, and a few seconds later he had jumped on to a bus going in the direction of the Place Vendôme.

For a good five minutes Maigret stood motionless on the curb, smoking his pipe.

9

A Pound of Ham

At the Quai des Orfèvres they were hunting upstairs and downstairs. Maigret was wanted urgently, as a message had come through from the *gendarmerie* at La Ferté-Alais.

Basso family found. Await instructions.

It was a typical case of scientific work supplemented by a stroke of luck.

First the scientific work: the examination of the tires on the Montlhéry track, which had reduced the probable area to the district of which La Ferté-Alais was the center.

But science took matters no further. In vain did the *gendarmes* search every hotel and inn of the neighborhood, in vain were a hundred people questioned.

In fact, the only result of the expert's work was that the local police could think of nothing else.

And on this Tuesday a certain *gendarme* named Piquart went home to lunch as usual.

"I forgot to get some onions this morning," said his wife, who was feeding her baby. "Would you mind running round to fetch some?"

A little country-town grocer's in the market-place. There were already four or five customers, all women, clustered at the counter. Piquart, who hated errands of this sort, stood aloof by the door. And, standing there, he heard the shopman's wife say to the old woman she was serving:

"You'll soon be getting fat with all the ham you're eating these days! A pound! And with only yourself to eat it."

Piquart looked without any particular interest at the old woman, a wizened creature who was known to all as Mère Mathilde. Poverty was written all over her. And then, while the ham was being cut, the *gendarme's* brain began to work. His own household consisted of three, yet they would never have thought of buying a pound of ham for a meal.

Abandoning his errand, he sneaked out of the shop, and followed Mère Mathilde to her home on the edge of the town, on the Ballancourt road, a cottage surrounded by a tiny garden in which hens were pickering about. He let her go in first, then knocked on the door and demanded admission in the name of the law.

Madame Basso, with an apron tied round her waist, was busy at the kitchen stove. On a rush-seated chair in a corner Basso was just opening the paper that Mère Mathilde had brought in with her. The boy was sitting on the floor playing with a puppy.

They telephoned to Maigret's flat in the Boulevard Richard-Lenoir and then tried various other likely places. It did not occur to them to ring up Basso's office on the Quai d'Austerlitz.

Yet that was where he went after James had left him. He was in a genial mood. His pipe between his teeth, and his hands in his pockets, he walked round the office, chatting and joking with the clerks. There being no instructions to the contrary, the business carried on exactly as before. On the quay, the cranes were in constant activity, unloading the barges of coal that arrived each day.

The offices were not modern. Not that they were ancient and dingy either. Taking a look round, it was easy to guess the way work was carried on.

For one thing, there was no private room for Basso. His desk was in one corner of the room, which also housed the chief accountant. His typist-secretary was at a desk near by.

Obviously Basso was not the man to stand on

his dignity. Altogether there was a free-and-easy atmosphere about the place, the clerks smoking over their ledgers.

"Yes, we have an address-book," answered the chief accountant to Maigret's enquiry, "but naturally it only contains business addresses. . . . Here it is, if you'd like to see it."

Maigret opened it at the U's, on the off-chance of finding Ulrich's name, and was not surprised when he failed to.

"Didn't he have a private address-book too?"

"I don't know of one."

"Weren't his private affairs ever seen to in the office? . . . For instance, when his son was born, weren't notices sent round to all his friends? . . . Who was here at that time? . . ."

"I was," said the secretary, a little reluctant to make the admission, for she was thirty-five and tried to look ten years younger.

"Who sent out the notices?"

"I did."

"Did he give you a list of addresses?"

"A little book."

"Where is it?"

She hesitated, wondering whether she ought to disclose Basso's private affairs. She turned to the chief clerk, who nodded, as much as to say:

"There's nothing for it but to do what he asks."

"It's in his desk at home," she answered submissively. "If you'll come with me . . ."

They went across the coal-yard. On the ground floor of the house, which was very simply furnished, was a study which looked as though it was never used. As a matter of fact, it was spoken of as the library.

The library of a family to whom reading did not mean very much. It was the place to keep anything that called itself a book, and that was about all. On one shelf were the prizes that Basso had won at school; on another, a series of bound numbers of the *Magazine des Familles*, dating fifty years back. Girls' books that Madame Basso had no doubt brought with her on her marriage. A number of yellow-backs bought on the strength of their advertisements. Lastly, some recent picture-books, belonging to the boy, whose toys filled up the shelves for which there were no books.

When the secretary opened a drawer of the desk, Maigret pointed to a large yellow envelope, sealed.

"What's that?"

"I believe it is monsieur's letters to madame when they were engaged."

"And the address-book?"

She looked in that drawer, then in another where there were nearly a dozen old pipes. Right at the back was the book they had come for. It was not really a proper address-book at all—just a little cheap notebook, that must have been at least fifteen years old. All the addresses were in Basso's writing, but it had changed with the years and the ink had faded.

It was rather like the seaweed cast up on the

foreshore, which reveals the tide that brought it by the degree it has withered.

A good many of the addresses dated from the earliest period. Friends of Basso's youth. How many of them would be remembered now? Some names were crossed out, as the result of a quarrel perhaps, or a death.

Several women's addresses, such as:

Lola, Bar des Eglantiers 18 Rue Montaigne.

But a line of thick blue chalk had eliminated Lola from Basso's life.

"Have you found what you wanted?" asked the secretary.

Yes. He had found it all right. A disreputable name that Basso hadn't even liked to write in full.

U. 13A, Rue des Blancs-Manteaux.

And both the writing and the faded ink showed this to be one of the earlier addresses too. Moreover, like so many of the others of its period, it had to be read through a thick stroke of blue chalk.

"Have you any idea when that address was written?"

"When Monsieur Basso was a young man and his father was still running the business."

"How do you know?"

"The ink's the same as the other addresses that are crossed out—the women's, I mean. Obviously they'd be before his engagement."

Maigret closed the little address-book and slipped it in his pocket, while the secretary looked at him reproachfully.

"Do you think he'll come back?" she asked, after a moment's hesitation.

The inspector confined his answer to a vague shrug of the shoulders.

When he arrived at the Quai des Orfèvres, he was told at once that they'd been looking for him, and as his heavy tread was heard in the corridor, his clerk, Jean, ran out to meet him.

"The Bassos have been found."

"Ah!"

Maigret sighed. Far from looking pleased, he seemed almost to take it as bad news.

"Has Lucas telephoned?"

"Twice. The man's still at the Salvation Army. He's up now. They've given him a meal and put him to do some cleaning."

"Is Janvier in?"

"I think he came in a few minutes ago."

Maigret went and found Janvier in another office.

"A thoroughly troublesome job for you, my boy. . . . I want you to hunt up a certain Lola who used to have her letters addressed to the *Bar des Eglantiers* some fifteen years ago, or possibly more."

"And since then?"

"Since then anything! She may be dead and

buried or have married an English lord. . . . It's up to you to find out."

In the train which took him to La Ferté-Alais he went through Basso's private address-book from cover to cover. More than once an indulgent, almost tender smile came on to his face, there were entries that spoke so eloquently of a man's wild oats.

The *lieutenant de gendarmerie* met him at the station and drove him to Mère Mathilde's house, in front of which Piquart was standing gravely on guard.

"We made sure there was no way of getting out by the back," explained the lieutenant. "And there's so little room inside, I thought it would be all right for him to be in the garden. . . . Shall I come in with you?"

"Perhaps not."

Maigret knocked, and the door was promptly opened. There was no hall, so he found himself stepping directly into the kitchen. It was getting late, and though still daylight outside, the window was so small that the figure in the room was little more than a shadow.

Basso sitting astride of a chair in the attitude of a man who has been waiting for hours and hours. No sign of his wife, who was doubtless in the next room with the boy.

"Can we have a light?" said Maigret to the old woman.

"I'll have to see first whether there's any oil in the lamp."

There was, and it was duly lit, the yellow flame gradually spreading till little by little its rays lit up the corners of the room.

It was very hot. A smell of poverty and country cottage.

"You can sit down again," said Maigret to Basso, and then to Mère Mathilde: "You can go into the next room, if you don't mind."

"What about my soup?"

"Run along! I'll see to that."

She went off, grumbling, and shut the door behind her. There was a murmur of voices in the next room.

"Are there only these two rooms?" asked the inspector.

"That's all. This and the bedroom."

"And you all slept there?"

"The two women and Pierrot. I managed in the corner here, on some straw."

Indeed, wisps of it were visible in the cracks between the uneven tiles. Basso was very calm, but with the sort of calmness that follows many days at fever-heat. It looked as though it was a relief to him to be arrested. In fact, the next thing he said was:

"I was going to give myself up."

He probably expected Maigret to look surprised, but the latter seemed to take it as the most natural thing in the world. He looked the coal-merchant over from head to foot.

"Isn't that one of James's suits?"

A gray lounge-suit. James was far from being of poor physique, but Basso was of a different build altogether, as broad and massive as Maigret himself. Few things can so belittle a man as a skimpy suit of clothes.

"There's no use denying it, if you know already."

"I know a good deal more than that, too. . . . But surely the soup doesn't need to go on boiling like that!"

Steam was puffing out of it, and the lid was dancing up and down. The air was heavy with soup. Maigret moved it to one side, his face being lit up by reddish flames till he put the ring in the hot plate.

"You knew Mère Mathilde?"

"I wanted to speak to you about her, and to ask you whether it would be possible to leave her out of it. She was a servant in my parents' house for many years. She knew me when I was little. And when I came here and asked her to hide me, she hadn't the heart to refuse."

"Of course not. But she might have had the sense not to go buying a pound of ham at a time."

Basso had lost weight. He looked a sorry sight, particularly since he hadn't shaved for several days.

"And I take it that my wife won't get into trouble either?"

He stood up awkwardly and fidgeted, obviously trying to compose his features and master his voice before launching out into the difficult subject that had to be discussed.

"Of course I was wrong," he began, "to remain in hiding so long. In fact, I ought never to have run away. It was the worst thing I could have done. But perhaps that's really in my favor. . . . At least, if I'd been a real criminal I wouldn't have been so stupid. As it was, I lost my head. The whole of my life had crumbled to ruins in a second. And all because of a trumpery little love-affair. . . . I had only one idea in my head: that I must get out of the country with my wife and son and start life over afresh."

"So you got James to bring them here, and also to cash a check for you. . . ."

"Yes."

"Only, it wasn't going to be so easy to get away, was it? You knew you were being hunted. . . ."

"Mathilde said she'd never seen so many *gendarmes* in her life."

They could hear noises from the next room—the boy scrambling about on the floor. Probably Madame Basso was listening at the door, for from time to time she said "Shhh," trying to hush him up.

"Today I came to the conclusion there was no other way out except to give myself up. But fate always seems to be against me. The *gendarme* got here first."

"Did you kill Feinstein or not?"

Basso looked fervently into Maigret's eyes.

"Yes . . . strictly speaking . . . I did," he said in a low quiet voice. "It's no use pretending I didn't. But I swear by all that's holy that what I'm going to tell you is the absolute truth. . . ."

"Just a moment!"

Maigret got up too. There they stood—two men of much the same build—under the low ceiling in the room that seemed too small for them.

"One question first: were you in love with Mado?"

Basso's lip curled with bitterness and disgust.

"Come on! You're a man too. Surely you can understand. . . . I'd known her for six or seven years—perhaps more. And all that time I'd never given her a thought. . . . Then one day . . . I hardly know myself just how it started. But some how or other I got kissing her, and then . . . at the bottom of the garden . . ."

"And after that?"

Basso sighed heavily. His shoulders drooped.

"She took it in earnest, swore she'd loved me all along and couldn't go on living without me. I'm no saint, and I know it's all my fault for starting it. But I never wanted to get tangled up in that way; I never wanted to risk breaking up my own home."

"So for that last year you've been meeting Mado secretly in Paris?"

"And she's been ringing me up every day. I've begged her again and again to be careful, but all to no purpose. She'd trump up any sort of pretext to ring me up again the very next day. . . . Oh, I knew the fat would be in the fire some day or other. . . . If only she hadn't been sincere! But I think she was genuinely in love with me. . . ."

"And Feinstein?"

"Yes," he groaned. "And Feinstein! That's why I couldn't bear the thought of facing a trial. There are limits to what one can say in court. There are limits to what public opinion will swallow. Can you see me in the witness-box—me, Mado's lover—accusing her husband of . . . ?"

"Of blackmailing you!"

"To start with, what proof have I? None whatever. You and I may call it blackmail, but he never threatened to expose me, never even showed he knew. . . . You remember him, don't you? So polite! Too polite! And always with that slightly sad smile of his. . . .

"The first time, he brought me some bill or other which he had to settle within twenty-four hours. He begged me to lend him the money, giving me all sorts of assurances. Well, I did what he asked . . . I should have done it in any case, quite apart from Mado. . . .

"Then he came to me again. And again after that. Until I tumbled to it that he was out to squeeze me systematically. I tried to wriggle out of it, and that's when the blackmail began.

"No threats. Just a heart-to-heart talk. He told me his wife was all he had to live for, that if he lived beyond his means it was only because he couldn't bear to refuse her anything, etc., etc.

"No. He'd rather kill himself than tell her she must go without something she wanted. And if he did, what would happen to her?

"It was always rather ambiguous. I hardly

ever knew precisely what he was driving at. Only I knew very well he was driving at something. And he nearly always managed to corner me, just after I'd been with Mado. In fact, I was often scared by the thought that her perfume might be hanging about my clothes. Once, while we were talking, he quite casually picked a hair off my shoulder and threw it on the ground. Of course it was Mado's.

"No, he wasn't the threatening sort, but the whining sort. And, my God! couldn't he whine! You can stand up against threats, because they make your blood boil. But what can you do with a man who weeps on you?

"Yes, he actually came and wept in my office. You've never heard such a pathetic story: 'You're young and strong,' he said. 'You've good looks, and what's more, you're rich. While I'm only . . .'

"And so he went on. It made me ill to listen to him. Yet even then I couldn't really swear he knew.

"Now for that Sunday . . .

"He had already spoken to me before playing bridge. He wanted fifty thousand francs urgently. . . . That's quite a lot of money, even if I am well off, and I said no, point-blank. Besides, I'd had about enough of it. And I told him if he bothered me again I'd refuse to have anything more to do with him.

"That's as far as it went then. But later on he maneuvered so as to cross the river with me. As soon as we were on the other side, he dragged me round to the back of the *Guinguette*.

"We were no sooner out of sight than he took that little revolver out of his pocket and pointed it at himself.

" 'This is what you condemn me to,' he said, 'and now all I ask is for you to take care of Mado!' "

Basso passed his hand across his forehead as though to wipe away the sordid memory.

"The whole thing was such rotten bad luck. I sprang forward to seize the revolver.

" 'No, no! It's too late now,' he cried, 'and it's your doing if I've come to this.' "

"Naturally he had no intention of doing it," grunted Maigret.

"I know. I'm sure of it. That's what makes it all so maddening. I was a fool. Of course I ought to have done nothing, and nothing would have happened. He'd merely have wept and changed his tune. But, no! I was too simpleminded. Just as I've been with Mado, just as I've always been with everything.

"I made a dash at him. He drew back, but I managed to seize his wrist and I wrenched the gun out of his hand.

"He tried to snatch it back. . . .

"And that's when it happened. I really don't know how. I didn't want him to get it, and I suppose my fingers closed on the trigger automatically. The next thing I knew was that it had gone off and Feinstein had fallen on the ground.

"He went down like a bag of sand, without a word, without a sigh.

"But who's going to believe me when I tell that to a jury? What shall I look like?

"A man who's killed his mistress's husband! And who then blackens the dead man's name by talking of blackmail."

He spoke violently, worked up by his own story. Then, more quietly, he went on:

"So I ran away. But as soon as I was here my one thought was to have it out with my wife, to tell her everything. And then to ask her whether . . . after all . . . she still . . .

"Mathilde bought a ready-made suit of clothes, saying it was a present for one of her nephews. I went up to Paris, knowing I'd find James at the *Taverne Royale.*

"James is a real friend. Perhaps the only one in the whole of our gang. . . .

"I don't think there's any more to tell you. My wife knows all. In a way it would have been better for everybody if we'd been able to slip out of the country. The trial's going to be a painful business for everybody. . . . With three hundred thousand francs I could easily make a fresh start—in Italy, for instance, or Egypt. I'm not afraid of hard work. . . .

"But . . . but do you believe my story?"

His face clouded suddenly as the misgiving entered his mind. He had been so absorbed by what he was saying that it had not occurred to him to question its credibility.

"I believe you killed Feinstein without intending to," Maigret answered slowly and emphatically.

"You see! . . ."

"Wait a moment! What I want to know is whether Feinstein hadn't something else to blackmail you with, besides his wife's infidelity. In other words . . ."

He paused for a moment to take the little address-book out of his pocket, opening it at the letter U.

"In other words, I want to know who, some six years ago, killed a certain Ulrich, a *brocanteur* in the Rue des Blancs-Manteaux, and threw the body into the Canal Saint-Martin. . . ."

He had to make an effort to finish the sentence, so deadly was the effect of the words, so staggering, so literally staggering that Basso's hand groped instinctively for support. The only thing it found was the stove, and he quickly withdrew it with an oath.

His eyes stared into Maigret's, stared with a look of horror. Then slowly he edged backwards, step by step, till, bumping into his chair, he collapsed into it.

"My God!"

And there he sat, inert, crushed, broken, senselessly repeating:

"My God!"

The door was flung open and Madame Basso rushed in, crying wildly:

"Marcel! . . . Marcel! . . . It isn't true, is it? Say it isn't true!"

He looked back at her, not understanding, perhaps not even seeing or hearing. And suddenly there was a choke in his voice—he took his head in his hands and burst into sobs. . . .

"Daddy! . . . Daddy! . . ."

Pierrot rushed in too, adding to the general confusion.

But Basso was beyond help, beyond consolation. He simply waved them away, waved away his wife, waved away his son.

Yes, he was crushed. That was the only word for it, his back rounded, his shoulders heaving spasmodically, the tears streaming down his cheeks.

The boy cried too. Madame Basso bit her lip and glared venomously at Maigret.

And the little old Mère Mathilde, not daring to come in, stood watching by the open door. She too was crying, crying as old people cry, with little regular sobs, and wiping her eyes with the corner of her check apron.

Till at last she too entered, trotting up to her stove. Still crying and snuffling, she poked up the fire, replaced the saucepan, and brought her soup once more up to the boil.

10

Maigret Slips Away

Scenes of that sort cannot last long. They soon play themselves out, doubtless because the nervous system cannot remain for any length of time strung up to such a pitch. The climax is no sooner reached than its reaction sets in, and a moment later the calm is as flat as the storm was frenzied.

And with the exhaustion comes shame, shame for the tears shed, the cries uttered, as though man had no business, no right to be emotional.

Maigret waited, ill at ease, gazing out of the little window at the *gendarme's* red *képi* in the blue-gray twilight. He was at the same time dimly conscious of all that went on in the room behind him, guessing the gestures from the words spoken—Madame Basso going up to her husband, taking him by the shoulders, and in a dead, hollow voice begging once again:

"Say it isn't true. . . ."

Basso sniffed, stood up, pushed her away, and looked round him with an almost drunken stare. The top of the stove was open, throwing a circle of red light on to the oak-beamed ceiling. Mathilde put on some more coal, and then replaced her soup.

The boy looked at his father, and in unconscious imitation stopped crying too.

"I'm sorry. . . . You mustn't mind. . . . It's all over now."

The voice was toneless. He was down, licked.

"Do you confess?"

"I've nothing to confess. . . . Listen. . . ."

He frowned as he looked at his family—a painful, wounded look.

"I didn't kill Ulrich. . . . If I broke down just now, it was because . . . because I . . ."

He hadn't even the energy to find his words.

"Because you couldn't prove your innocence."

He nodded, then repeated:

"But I didn't kill him."

"You said the same thing immediately after Feinstein's death, yet from what you've just told me . . ."

"It's not the same thing."

"You knew Ulrich, didn't you?"

A bitter smile.

"Look at the date on the fly-leaf of the address-book. Fifteen years ago. And it's something like ten since I saw Old Ulrich for the last time. . . ."

He was more composed now, though his voice betrayed the same despair.

"My father was still living then. . . . Ask anybody about my father. They'll all tell you the same thing. A strict man, hard on himself and on others. In fact, I was allowed less pocket-money than the poorest of my friends. . . . One of them gave me Old Ulrich's address in the Rue des Blancs-Manteaux. Young men who wanted a bit of money for a fling were just in his line."

"And you never knew of his death?"

Basso said nothing, and Maigret hammered out the words a second time:

"You never knew of his death? Never knew he'd been killed, then taken in a car and thrown into the Canal Saint-Martin?"

Basso still said nothing. Only, his shoulders drooped a shade more than before. He looked at his wife, at his son, and at the old family servant, who, still crying, began automatically to lay the table because it was supper-time.

"What are you going to do?"

"I'm going to arrest you. Madame Basso and the boy can stay here or go home, whichever you prefer. . . ."

Then, opening the door, Maigret said to the *gendarme:*

"Call me a car."

There were two or three little groups of onlookers outside, but they kept their distance like the cautious peasants they were. When Maigret turned round, Madame Basso was in her husband's arms, the latter mechanically tapping her on the back while staring into vacancy.

"You'll look after yourself, won't you? And, above all, promise me you won't do anything foolish."

"Yes. . . ."

"You promise?"

"Yes. . . ."

"It's for your son's sake, Marcel!"

"Yes . . ." he said for the third time, with a touch of exasperation in his voice.

Perhaps it was as much as he could stand. Perhaps he was afraid of collapsing again. He broke away from her, and stood fidgeting, waiting impatiently for the car he'd heard Maigret order, in the meantime wanting only to say nothing, see nothing, and hear nothing. But he wasn't to be left in peace.

"You didn't kill that man, did you? . . . Listen, Marcel! You must listen to me. . . . For . . . for the other one, they can't possibly convict you. It was an accident, and they're bound to see it. And we can prove that Feinstein was a cad. . . . I'll get hold of a lawyer at once—somebody absolutely first-rate. . . ."

She spoke passionately. She was determined he should hear.

"Everybody knows you're an honest man.

And they'll probably let you out on bail. Don't let yourself be discouraged—that's the most important thing of all. . . . And since the other . . . the other crime wasn't your doing . . ."

She threw a defiant look at Maigret.

"I'll see a lawyer tomorrow morning. . . . I'll ask Father to come over from Nancy. He'll be a great help. . . . We've got to fight this, Marcel. You're not going to give in, are you?"

She didn't realize she was hurting him, that the only effect her words could have was to sap the little strength left to him. He was struggling not to hear, focusing all his attention outside, listening for the arrival of the longed-for car.

"I'll come and see you . . . with Pierrot. . . ."

At last it came, the purr of an engine, and Maigret cut the scene short.

"Come on!"

"Remember, Marcel, you've promised. . . ."

She couldn't bear to let him go. She pushed the boy towards his father to make doubly sure of the promise she had extorted. But Basso was already going down the three steps outside the door.

Then she seized Maigret's arm, so violently that she hurt him.

"Look out!" she panted. "Look out he doesn't kill himself. I know the sort of man he is. . . ."

She caught sight of the staring onlookers and stared back boldly and shamelessly.

"Marcel! . . . Your scarf! . . ."

She fetched it from indoors, ran down the

garden path and pushed it through the window just as the car was starting.

In the car, Basso breathed more freely. They were only men together now, and that made it easier. For a good ten minutes, however, neither spoke. It was not till they left the *route departmentale* and turned into the main road to Paris that Maigret said simply:

"A grand woman, that!"

"Yes. . . . She understands. . . . And to think I could risk losing her by fooling around with . . . with Mado!"

Another silence. Then he went on quietly, in a confidential tone:

"At the time, you simply don't think. . . . It's just a game, then a bit more than a game, and you haven't quite got the courage to break it off. You're afraid of a scene. . . . And this is what comes of it. . . ."

The scenery consisted of nothing but trees on either hand, which swept by in the glare of the head-lamps. Maigret filled his pipe, and passed his pouch to his companion.

"Thanks. But I only smoke cigarettes."

It was good to talk of things like that, little everyday matters.

"Go on! I saw something like a dozen pipes in a drawer of your desk."

"Yes. . . . I used to. In fact, I was mad about pipes. But my wife didn't like it, and . . ."

Even this subject was difficult. The voice had faltered over the last sentence. Maigret hastily switched on to something else.

"Your secretary—I should think she's very devoted to you."

"She's a good sort. Yes, devoted's the word. I suppose she's fearfully upset about this?"

"Not fearfully. She seems quite sure you'll be back before long."

They relapsed into silence again. The car was running through Juvisy. At Orly the searchlights of the aerodrome swept the sky.

"Was it you who gave Feinstein Ulrich's address?"

But Basso was on his guard at once. He didn't answer.

"Feinstein dealt with him pretty regularly. The sums are entered up in his books. At the time of the moneylender's death he owed him thirty-three thousand francs. . . ."

Basso made no response. And there was something obstinate about his silence, as though he was determined not to be drawn out.

"What is your father-in-law by profession?"

"Schoolmaster. He's in a *lycée* in Nancy. My wife was trained as a teacher too."

So the conversation ebbed and flowed, constantly approaching the danger-line and then receding into harmless small talk. At times Basso was speaking almost naturally, as though forgetting the situation he was in; at others there were sudden tense silences, heavy with unspoken misgivings.

"Your wife's quite right. You've a good chance of being acquitted as regards the Feinstein affair.

At the most they couldn't give you more than a year. . . . But as for the other business . . ."

Then, abruptly turning to practical matters:

"We'll keep you for the time being in the *Police Judiciaire,* and hand you over to the *Sûreté* later on."

Maigret knocked out his pipe and slid the front window aside to say to the driver:

"Quai des Orfèvres. Drive straight into the yard."

There was no fuss, no formalities to be gone through. Maigret led Basso to the cell where Victor Gaillard had been locked up, glancing round to see that all was in order.

"Good night," he said finally. "I'll see you in the morning. You're quite sure there's nothing you want to tell me now?"

Was Basso too moved to answer? Anyhow, he merely looked down, shaking his head.

Confirm arrival tomorrow morning by night train. Staying some days. Love.

It was on Wednesday morning that Maigret wired again to his wife. He was sitting at his desk at the Quai des Orfèvres, and he sent Jean out with the telegram to the post office.

A few moments later he was telephoning to the examining magistrate who was in charge of the Feinstein case.

"This evening, I hope to make you a full report on it. . . . Yes. It's all cut and dried. Culpable homicide at the most. Nothing in the least interesting. . . . Yes. . . . Very well, then, I'll come round this evening."

He went into the next room, where he found Lucas writing up a report.

"How about Victor?"

"Dubois relieved me. . . . I'm just making out the report. . . . I told you he was working at the Salvation Army place..Well, he seemed to be settling down to it in earnest. He'd talked about his lungs, of course, so they were full of consideration. No doubt they looked upon him as a sure recruit. In fact, I was getting quite used to the idea of seeing him in a month's time in a uniform with a red collar. . . ."

"And then?"

"It didn't last long. Yesterday evening one of the officers arrived in the place and told him to do something. I don't know what it was, but evidently it was something Victor hadn't bargained for. He refused, and kicked up the deuce of a scene, saying it was disgraceful to make a one-lunged man work like a dog. . . . They asked him to go, but he wouldn't, and then of course they chucked him out. Quite a pretty little scuffle. . . . He spent the night under the Pont-Marie. When Dubois took over, he was wandering along the quays. . . . Dubois will be ringing up at lunchtime to keep you informed. . . ."

"I shan't be here, so when he does will you give him a message? Tell him to bring Victor round here and lock him up in the same cell he was in before, *with the man that's there now.*"

"Right!"

At the door, Maigret turned round.

"By the way! You can tell Janvier not to bother about Lola."

"Lola?"

"Yes. He'll know. Tell him I don't think we shall want her after all."

He went home, fished out some country clothes, and packed his bag. He had lunch in a *brasserie* near the Place de la République, where he also called for a timetable to make sure of his train, the 12.10 from the Gare de l'Est.

He sat on for a long time after the meal, reading newspapers, then walked, or rather dawdled about, filling in the time till five o'clock, when he punctually took his customary seat at the *Taverne Royale.* He had not been there many minutes when James joined him, holding out his hand, looking round for the waiter, and asking:

"Pernod?"

"*Ma foi! . . .*"

"Waiter! Two Pernods!"

James sat down, crossed his legs, and sighed, staring in front of him like a man who has nothing to say, nor even anything to think. The sky was gray. Unexpected gusts of wind swept along the streets, blowing up clouds of dust.

"We'll be having another storm," sighed James.

Then, without any transition:

"Is it true—what the papers say? Have you really arrested Basso?"

"Yesterday afternoon."

"Here's how! It's absurd. . . ."
"What is?"
"The way he's behaved. Look at him! A substantial, respectable man with every reason to feel sure of himself. And then to go and lose his head like a child. I thought for a moment he might have some reason. But obviously he'd have done far better to stand his ground and face the music."
So James was taking the same line as Madame Basso. Somehow Maigret couldn't help smiling.
"Here's how! . . . You may be right, but you may equally be wrong. It all depends. . . ."
"What do you mean? You're not going to tell me that Basso meant to kill Feinstein, are you? And if he didn't mean to, you can't, by any stretch, call it a crime."
"I quite agree. That is, if he's nothing on his conscience besides Feinstein's death. But . . ."
And with startling abruptness he called out:
"Waiter! How much is that?"
"Six francs fifty."
"Are you going?"
"Yes. I've got to see Basso."
"Ah!"
"For that matter . . . if you'd like to come too, I'll take you along with me. . . . You'd like to see him, wouldn't you?"
Nothing was said in the taxi till they were halfway there. Then James asked:
"How did Madame Basso take it?"
"She's a remarkable woman. Any amount of pluck. And it seems she's cultured too. I never

suspected it, seeing her at Morsang in sailor clothes. . . . And how's your wife?"

"Very well, thanks. Just as usual."

"She hasn't been worried by all this trouble?"

"Why should she be? . . . Besides, she's not really the worrying sort. She's generally thinking about the housework or her sewing, or what she's going to buy in the sales. . . ."

"Here we are. Come along with me."

He led James across the yard. Coming to the man on guard outside the cell, he asked:

"Are they both there?"

"Yes."

"Quiet?"

"The one Dubois brought in made a bit of a row, talking about his rights, and saying he'd get his case taken up by some society or other."

Maigret hardly smiled. Opening the door, he pushed James in front of him.

There was only one bed in the cell, of which Victor had taken possession, having first discarded his jacket and shoes. Basso was walking up and down with his hands behind his back. For a second he glanced enquiringly at James, then his eyes shifted to Maigret.

As for Victor Gaillard, he raised himself, scowled, then lay down again, muttering unintelligibly.

"Glad to see you, James . . ." said Basso, offering his hand.

It was meant to be cordial. But there was something wrong, though it was difficult to say what. Something unexpressed which nevertheless cast a chill over the atmosphere, and which perhaps made Maigret think that what he wanted was not going to come of itself.

Anyhow, he decided to come straight to the point.

"Gentlemen," he said, "I must ask you to sit down, for I've something to say which may take a little time. . . . Here, you! Make room on the bed. And just see if you can't go a quarter of an hour without coughing. It won't be any use to you here."

Victor contented himself with a supercilious grin, like a man who's biding his time.

"Sit down, James. You too, Monsieur Basso. . . . That's better. . . . If you'll listen to me, I'll try to sum up the situation as concisely as possible. Now, if you're quite ready. . . .

"A few months ago a man called Lenoir was sentenced to death. I saw him the day before his execution, and he told me about a certain crime. He mentioned no names—except the Christian name of our friend here—and he would never have said what he did if he'd thought it could give anybody away.

"Six years ago a car drove off from a house in Paris and stopped by the Canal Saint-Martin. The driver then left his seat, fished a corpse out of the back of his car, and threw it into the water.

"A crime whose very simplicity left no trace, and nothing would ever have been known of it if there hadn't been two witnesses, two crooks whose names were Lenoir and Victor Gaillard, who accompanied him the whole way on the back of the car.

"Being the sort they were, they didn't come to the police. They preferred to turn their knowledge into hard cash for themselves. So they called on the driver of the car and squeezed him periodically, for as much as they dared ask.

"But they were new to the game and did not take sufficient precautions. One day their victim had moved, without leaving an address behind him.

"That's all as far as the crime's concerned, except that the body was that of a Jewish *brocanteur* called Ulrich, who was really a moneylender."

The inspector slowly lit his pipe without looking at the others. Nor did he look at them in the conversation that followed, except now and again when he snapped at Victor.

"Six years later, quite by chance, Lenoir came across the murderer. But he had no opportunity to renew business dealings, for another crime he had committed sent him to the guillotine.

"But listen to this. . . . Before his execution he talked to me about the murder. He didn't say a great deal, but it was just enough to give me a useful hint. And before his death he managed to send word to Victor to announce his discovery. At this news, Victor promptly left his sanatorium and hastened to the *Guinguette à Deux Sous*.

"Which brings us to the second act. . . . No, James, don't interrupt me. Nor you either, Victor.

"On the Sunday of Feinstein's death, Ulrich's murderer was at the *Guinguette.* It might have been you, Basso, or you, James, or Feinstein himself, or even one of the others. Someone was there who was recognized by Victor. . . .

"And Victor's the only one who can tell us who it was."

The latter opened his mouth to speak, and Maigret literally shouted:

"Silence!"

Then, in the same quiet tone as before, he went on:

"But it happens that this Victor, besides being a dirty little toad, is a shrewd little fox. He also has the advantage of having only one lung—but we'll let that pass. . . . Anyhow, he has no intention of giving anything away for nothing. His price is thirty thousand francs, or to be quite precise, twenty-five thousand. That's his lowest figure. . . . *Silence, sacrebleu!* Will you let me finish? . . .

"The police is not accustomed to doling out sums of that magnitude, and we've no way of putting pressure on a one-lunged man. . . .

"I said just now that it might have been one of three present, or any of the others. But that's not to say that everybody is equally suspicious. For instance, we know that Basso knew Ulrich at one time and had dealings with him. The same of Feinstein, only in his case we know still more—that at the time of the moneylender's death he owed him thirty-three thousand francs, a debt which lapsed with the murder.

"Feinstein's dead. Enough has come to light to show he was a distinctly undesirable person. If he killed Ulrich, that closes the case. . . .

"But did he? . . . Victor could tell us in a second, but I'm not in a position to pay him twenty-five thousand for the information. . . .

"*Silence, sacrebleu!* . . . You can hold your tongue until you're spoken to."

Victor was fidgeting all the time. He was simply dying to get a word in.

Maigret looked at the floor. He had been speaking in a dull, monotonous voice, almost as if he'd been reciting a lesson.

Suddenly he jumped up and made for the door, muttering:

"Just a moment! I must ring somebody up. I'll be back in a moment."

His steps faded away in the distance.

11

The Settlement

Maigret sat at his desk telephoning. He had the examining magistrate at the other end of the line.

"Yes, *Monsieur le juge,*" he said finally, "within the next ten minutes or so. . . . Who? . . . I tell you, I don't know yet. . . . No, it's not a joke. Am I in the habit of pulling your leg? . . ."

He rang off, walked two or three times up and down his room, then went up to Jean.

"I'm catching the 12.10 tonight and shan't be back for a few days. Here's my address."

Several times he looked at his watch, finally leaving the room and going downstairs to the cell where he had left the three men boxed up together.

The first thing he saw as he went in was Victor, with fury and discomfiture written all over his face. He was no longer sitting on the bed, but raging up and down the cell. Basso was still sitting where Maigret had left him, only now he was holding his head between his hands.

As for James, he was standing with his arms folded, leaning against the wall, while he looked at Maigret with a strange smile.

"I'm sorry to keep you waiting. I . . ."

"It's all over," broke in James. "It would have been anyhow. Your absence wasn't necessary."

His smile grew still stranger as Maigret lost countenance.

"Victor Gaillard won't earn his twenty-five thousand either by talking or holding his tongue. . . . It was I who killed Old Ulrich."

The inspector opened the door and called the policeman who was on guard outside.

"Take this man away"—he pointed at Victor—"and shut him up anywhere you like till I've finished here."

But the wretch could not resign himself to failure.

"Don't forget who put you on Ulrich's track," he whined. "Without that, where would you be? . . . And it's well worth . . ."

Maigret no longer wanted to bash his face in, Victor's futile obstinacy was now merely pitiable.

"Five thousand," Victor shouted over his shoulder as he was dragged away.

* * *

And so they were left, the three men, in the special cell of the *Police Judiciaire*. Of the three, Basso was by far the most upset. He remained sitting where he was during a silence that must have lasted a full minute. Then he rose to his feet and, standing before Maigret, said:

"Please don't think I'd have let him down, Inspector. I'd have given the twenty-five thousand willingly. What's twenty-five thousand to me compared to . . . ? But James wouldn't let me. . . ."

Maigret looked from one to the other. He too was upset. Somehow the scene wasn't at all what he'd pictured. With the surprise that was plainly written on his face was also a sympathy that was almost affectionate.

"I suppose you knew, Basso?"

"All along," murmured the coal-merchant. Then James explained:

"It was Basso who gave me the money to keep them quiet. Of course I had to tell him everything. . . ."

"And after all these years to chuck up the sponge for a matter of twenty-five thousand!"

"It's not that. . . . You can't understand, nor the inspector either."

His eye wandered, as though looking for something.

"Has anybody got a cigarette?"

Basso held out his case.

"No Pernod, I'm afraid. Never mind! I shall

have to get used to that. All the same, it would have made things easier."

His lips moved like those of a drinker tormented by his craving.

"There isn't a lot to be said. . . . I was comfortably married and leading the same quiet little life as anybody else. Then I ran into Mado, and like a fool I thought the great moment had come. Just like a novelette. *My life for a kiss. Live dangerously*. And all the rest. My quiet little life seemed merely squalid."

The phlegmatic and slightly contemptuous way he spoke made his confession sound almost unreal, inhuman. But then James looked like a clown, anyhow.

"I was just at the right age to get it badly. Secret meetings in a secret room. Cakes and glasses of port in *pâtisseries*. And there was nothing cheap about it—at least, not to a clerk earning a thousand francs a month. Of course I didn't dare let on to Mado that I couldn't afford it.

"I was caught. And instead of breaking free, I simply plunged in all the deeper, just as millions have before me. Not a very original story. The only amusing thing about it is that it was my mistress's husband who gave me Ulrich's address."

"Did you borrow a lot?"

"Less than seven thousand. But that's quite enough when a chap's only earning a thousand a month. . . . Then one night Ulrich came to see me. My wife was at Vendôme at her sister's. He said if I couldn't pay back the loans I must at any rate pay the interest on them. If I didn't, he'd go to my employers and tell them—and also put the bailiffs on me."

James still spoke in the same calm, disdainful tone.

"That meant the end of everything. I saw red. As a matter of fact, I only wanted to frighten him, but as soon as I hit him he tried to call for help. Then I took him by the throat. . . . All the same, I was as cool and collected as could be. It's a great mistake to think one necessarily loses one's head at such moments. I did nothing of the kind. In fact, I doubt if I've ever been more lucid in my life. . . . I went out and hired a car, pinching some of the tools to put into Ulrich's pockets. Then I carried him down as though he was a drunk, talking to him as I went. . . . You know the rest."

He took a hand out of his pocket, then stuffed it back again. He had almost reached out automatically for the glass that wasn't there!

"That's all. . . . After a thing like that, life looks different. The Mado affair dragged on for another month or so. My wife got into the habit of going at me for drinking—for that's when I started. . . .

"And then the two crooks who started squeezing me . . . I couldn't pay them, any more than I could pay Ulrich his interest. The only person I could turn to was Basso, so I went and told him the whole story. . . . They say it does you good to confess, but, believe me, all that's just storybook stuff. Nothing does any good. The only thing that could do any good would be to begin all over again. Right from the start. Right from the cradle."

The words sounded so incongruous in James's drawling, disdainful voice, that Maigret couldn't help smiling. And he noticed that they brought a faint smile even to Basso's distraught face.

"Stupid, wasn't it? Only, it would have been stupider still to go round to the police station and say you'd killed a man."

"So you just bottled it up," said Maigret. "And looked round for some place you could call your own. . . ."

"One has to get through life somehow. . . ."

A hopeless story. An endless stretch of dreary desolation that lacked the climax of a real tragedy. But James didn't want it to be tragic. He made it a point of honor to remain simple and matter-of-fact whatever happened. Nor was this a pose—just a natural distaste for giving way to feelings.

In the end, he was much the calmest of the three, and his quizzical eye seemed to be wondering what on earth there was to be so troubled about.

"Really, men are fools! To think that Basso should go and put his head in a noose too! And with Mado of all people! Yes, it had to be Mado!

"If I'd had a chance I'd have said I killed Feinstein myself. There'd have been some use in that. And it would . . . it would have settled things. . . . But as luck would have it, I had an inspector of the *Police Judiciaire* to witness that I didn't. . . .

"And of course Basso did the worst thing possible. He bolted. . . . I did what I could to help. . . ."

There was, after all, a little quaver in James's voice, and it was only after a long pause that he went on in the same monotonous drawl as before:

"He ought to have told the truth straight away. But he has a genius for getting in a mess. Just now he wanted to give Victor his twenty-five thousand."

"It would have been the best way out," growled Basso. "Now . . ."

"Now we've got things settled for good and all. I wash my hands of everything. Of this pettifogging existence, of the bank, of the *Taverne Royale*, of . . ."

He broke off. He had nearly said:

". . . of my wife."

Of the wife with whom he had nothing in common. Of the little studio-like flat in the Rue Championnet to which he'd return shortly after eight each day, to while away the evening dipping idly into any book that came to hand, with her sewing in the opposite corner.

"This way," he went on, "this way I shall be left in peace."

In prison. Or in a convict settlement. Another place to call his own!

A place where things would be settled once

and for all. No longer anything to hide, nor anything to expect. A place where he would keep regular hours, getting up, going to bed, having meals, breaking stones by the roadside or making knick-knacks in the prison workshops.

"I suppose it'll be twenty years, won't it?"

Basso looked at him. But he could hardly see him for the tears that were welling up in his eyes and rolling down his cheeks.

"Stop it, James! Stop it!" he pleaded, wringing his hands.

"Why should I?"

Maigret blew his nose, then absentmindedly lit a match to light his pipe, forgetting that he had not filled it.

He had the feeling he had never been so far along the dreary road of desolation and black despair.

No, not even black! An endless stretch of grayness, devoid of all struggle, all resentment, unbroken by either protest or complaint.

A drunkard's despair, but without intoxication.

And suddenly Maigret understood the nature of the bond between him and James, the bond which had kept them hour after hour side by side on the terrace of the *Taverne Royale*.

They had drunk their Pernods, saying little, staring out at the passing traffic. And all the time, in his heart of hearts, James had been hoping that his companion would one day bring his heavy hand down on his shoulder, the heavy hand of the law which settled everything!

He had loved Maigret as a friend and a deliverer. Once again Maigret had been called to the rescue.

Maigret and Basso exchanged glances, unfathomable glances. Meanwhile James squashed the end of his cigarette on the top of the deal table, saying:

"The trouble is, it takes so long to get there. Endless questioning and writing out statements. . . . Then the trial. . . . People who break down or try to console you. . . ."

A detective opened the door.

"The examining magistrate's here," he announced.

Maigret hesitated, not knowing quite how to deal with the situation. But James came up to him and took him by the arm.

"Look here," he said. "Do me a good turn, will you? Ask him to push it through as quickly as he can. I'll confess anything he likes, so long as they send me off to my little corner as speedily as possible."

And to finish off on the right note, he deliberately went on:

"The chap I'm sorry for is the waiter at the *Taverne Royale*. He'll miss me all right. But perhaps you'll take my place from time to time, Inspector. . . ."